'I want to *do* [illegible]g Matt!'

'We've done a lot of things.'

He ticked off the items with his fingers.

'We've mended your brother's side-car, had a Chinese lunch – '

'Take away.'

Matt shrugged.

'Had a take away Chinese lunch which we had to eat in the car. What's so wrong with that?'

'You were driving rather fast at the time.'

Forty miles an hour to be absolutely accurate.

'Well you said you wanted to go round Hyde Park.'

'On *foot*.'

'There was nowhere to park this side of Birmingham. You fed the ducks.'

'Throwing bread from a moving car roughly in the direction of the Round Pond is not my idea of feeding the ducks.'

Matt shook his head. He didn't like to point out to Lily that it was hardly his fault that he was allergic to feathers, any more than it was his fault that she was not a very accurate long distance duck feeder. . . .

Also by Terence Brady and Charlotte Bingham and available from Sphere

ROSE'S STORY

Yes – Honestly

TERENCE BRADY and
CHARLOTTE BINGHAM

SPHERE BOOKS LIMITED
30/32 Gray's Inn Road, London WC1X 8JL

First published in Great Britain by Sphere Books Ltd 1977

From the London Weekend Television series
starring Donal Donnelly and Liza Goddard

TRADE
MARK

Set in Monotype Baskerville

Printed in Great Britain by
Hunt Barnard Printing Ltd
Aylesbury, Bucks

Being the story of Matt and Lily

TO HUMPHREY

CHAPTER ONE

Will the real Lionel Blanchard please stand up?

Matt was getting cramp. Which was hardly surprising, since crouching on one's haunches under a covered table in the sitting room of your own flat for nigh on one hour more or less guarantees an attack of some sort of rigor. Fortunately there was a small hole torn in the all-concealing floor length tablecloth, through which Matt was able to observe the movements of the object from which he was hiding, and thus distract himself from the spasmodic tic which was presently convulsing his thigh muscles. He shifted himself carefully for another progress report. No – unhappily the nightmare object was still very much at large in his flat, inhaling clouds of revolting cigarette smoke and helping herself to generous measures of his precious malt whisky. His blood pressure shot up another two points. If there was one thing he abhorred more than a smoking woman, it was a smoking *and* drinking woman, particularly one who drank his precious whisky. In fact Matt was coming to the conclusion that perhaps he hated women full stop. He certainly had not yet found one that he actually *liked.* He may have desired many, he may have admired many, but he had never yet found himself in that most upsetting of circumstances, which was to be thinking constantly more about another person than you do about yourself. And the way he felt presently about the female person presently desecrating his beautiful flat with her odious presence only added to his growing suspicion that he was fast becoming a confirmed misogynist.

The female object of his current animosity (a very large square bodied human named Peggy Northolt) gave sudden vent to a deep exhalation of disgust and impatience, then stubbed out her cigarette in a plate of petit fours. The spying Matt controlled his growing fury in the hope that such an action signalled her intention to throw in the towel and depart. But no such luck. Through his spyhole he saw her lower her vast frame into his favourite armchair and light another Woodbine. *Women*, he thought. Thomas Dekker was right. Were there no women, men might live like Gods.

Then his doorbell rang. Matt frowned. And *who* could this be? He wasn't expecting anybody else. He shifted his position so that he could watch the dread Peggy answer the door, but to no avail, because the sofa was directly in his eyeline. He heard the door open.

'And where in hell have *you* been?' demanded dread Peg, obviously assuming the bell ringer to be him.

'Been?' came a rather squeaky reply. 'I've only just arrived.'

The new voice was female. Matt closed his eyes and sighed. Two women in one day was two too many. Perhaps she was just delivering something.

'I have an appointment,' said the new voice, tremulously.

An appointment?

'And much good may it do you,' answered dread Peg, marching back centre stage. Matt had her in his sights again. Would that he were a submarine and she an enemy destroyer. He lined up a torpedo.

'Sorry,' came the new voice, 'but I am a bit late. No, not really late as such. More missing presumed lost. Eh alors.'

And with that she crossed right into Matt's sights, thus robbing him of the chance of a direct hit on HMS Northolt. He tried to make out what the owner of the new voice looked like, but all he could distinguish was a large all enveloping yellow cycling cape which was busily dripping today's rain on his carpets, and the back view of an oversize sou'wester.

'Now then,' said the cape, unloading a mass of trivia from a brown paper carrier bag on to the top of Matt's precious piano, thus almost causing his second near heart attack of the day. 'Now then – who exactly am I looking for? For whom exactly am I looking?'

The sou'wester consulted a scrap of paper in the cape's hand.

'I seem to be searching for a Mr – Bosom,' it continued. 'No. No I don't think I'm looking for a Bosom.'

'It's Browne,' said dread Peg flatly.

'Of course it's brown,' said the cape, waving the list in its hand. 'It's wrapping paper.'

'It is Mr Browne for whom you search.'

'Oh. Ta muchly,' replied the cape. 'That makes me feel a lot better.'

And with that it unloaded even more goods on to the top of the Steinway in order to gain access to its box of tissues, which like everything else needed urgently always lies at the bottom of the pile.

It sneezed.

'Sorry. Is Mr Browne about?'

'God knows what he is about,' growled dread Peg. 'I disappeared to powder me nose and the next thing I hear is the demented imbecile shouting that he's just popping out to the chemist.'

'Oh well,' shrugged the cape.

'Sixty-five minutes ago,' retorted dread Peg.

'Really? The chemists was probably further away than he remembered,' proffered the cape. 'Shops always are when it's raining.'

Matt sank back on his heels in despair. From the sound of the banter they could be here all day. Then suddenly the US cavalry arrived.

'I am going home,' announced Peggy.

Not only the cavalry but the marines as well. Matt nearly stood up and cheered.

'Why anyone ever thought we could actually *work* together,' continued dread Peg, packing up her briefcase, 'God knows.'

'You work together, do you?' asked the cape, also – as Matt was pleased to observe – repacking its belongings in its supermarket hold-all. 'What do you do?'

'I am Peggy Northolt. A writer.'

'A *writer*?' gasped the cycling cape, awestruck.

'*The* writer.'

'Môche!' continued the cape. ' "And what sin unknown dipped you in ink? Your parents or your own?" '

Peggy finished her packing, then drew herself upright.

'Neither,' she replied. 'I just didn't make it as a full time person.'

She closed her case and started to move to the door.

'Is Mr Whatsit a writer too?'

'No. No, Mr "Whatsit" is a composer. But from what I know of him mysogynistic maniac is a more befitting number plate. Have you not *met* Mr Browne?'

'Crikey no, Miss Heathrow – '

'*Northolt.*'

'I'm only here to pick up his typing.'

My typing? mused Matt. But that's never Mrs Grey. He peered out again to try and identify the cape, but the protagonists were again by the door.

'Tell him I couldn't wait,' said dread Peg. 'In fact you can tell him to – '

'I'll just tell him you couldn't wait,' said the mystery voice tactfully and closed the door.

There was a moment's silence, then Matt saw the yellow mackintosh trudge back into view and across to his piano.

'Some drum,' it muttered as the sou'wester took in its surroundings. Then it produced an apple from its carrier and moved closer to the keyboard. Its right hand essayed a few notes.

'And some joanna.'

This is getting *too* much, thought Matt. Too much altogether. Have people no respect for other people's property anymore? He looked through his spyhole and saw the cape now sitting at the piano about to play.

' "Blue moon",' it warbled, vamping discordantly with its left hand, ' "You saw me standing alone, You knew just what I was there for . . ." '

Matt could take it no more.

'No!' he cried.

The singing stopped at once as the sou'wester tried to locate the sudden interruption. Then it continued.

' "Without a love of my own,

' "Blue moon – " '

'Will you leave that piano alone!' Matt howled.

'Nom de chien,' muttered the cape.

'That is not a vehicle for vamping!'

The cape stood up and peered anxiously around the room, totally unable to place the voice.

After a moment it queried:
'Where are you?'
'It doesn't matter where I am!' Matt replied irritably. '*Who* are *you*?'
'Swop,' said the cape. 'Your location for my designation.'
Matt remained silent. He was damned if he was going to give away his bolt hole.
'Je suis only la teepist, monsieur,' continued the baffled cyclist. 'I'm the temp who's come to collect your typing.'
'So where's Mrs Grey?'
'Mrs Grey?' replied the cape, playing for time, 'Mrs Grey's got the blues, Mr Browne.'
It paused, hoping for a laugh, or a snort, or any such reaction that would help her place where the maniac lay hidden.
'The typing is on the coffee table,' said the voice suddenly. 'And I want it back by tomorrow.'
'On the coffee table.'
'Now if you don't mind,' continued the voice, watching carefully as the cape picked up the folder, 'I have work to do.'
'Okay.'
Matt saw to his vast relief the yellow cape move towards the door.
'Going.'
'Good-bye.'
'But I am sure there's something I've forgotten,' it muttered, out of sight now by the door.
'Good-*bye*,' Matt reaffirmed.
'Good-bye,' it said, then paused at the open door. 'You can come out from under the table now.'
And then it was gone.
After a moment, when he was sure the coast was clear, Matt lifted the cloth and looked out at his now empty flat.
'Women,' he exclaimed passionately. '*Women*.'

It wasn't until much later in the day that Lily Pond, the owner of the cape and sou'wester, discovered what she had left at the invisible Mr Browne's. She was busily doing her very best to type out her temporary employer's letters on her reconditioned Japanese portable when her mother knocked on her bedroom door, causing her to mistype yet again the comparatively simple phrase, 'Dear Sir'.

'Yes?' she sighed in answer to the knock, at the same time consigning yet another battle-scarred sheet of paper to the basket, 'What is it now?'

'Lily?' said her mother pushing open the door. 'I only wanted to know if you wanted a mug of hot chocolate. I'm making one for your grandmother.'

Lily selected a clean sheet of paper and put it in her typewriter.

'A *mug* of hot chocolate?' she said derisively. 'When I have sold my masterpiece, Ma, we shall be drinking our nightcaps out of the finest Spode.'

'Spode indeed,' sniffed her mother, coming in and casting a maternal eye around her daughter's bedroom. 'When you are rich and famous, Lily Pond, the first thing you can do is buy us some decent china. So. How are you doing?'

'I'm not. I have to do all these boring letters, yawn yawn. No creative work ce soir.'

'I thought you were working on your play.'

'Smatteroffact, Ma,' replied Lily, 'I finished my play at the week-end.' She peered at the letter she was meant to be typing. 'C'est tout finis. Fin-fin. Shaftesbury Avenue here I come.'

She started to type again while her mother sadly regarded her back.

'Oh well,' said Mrs Pond, sitting down on the bed. 'I suppose you had to think of leaving home some day.'

'Leaving home?' said Lily, adding another dose of snow-flake to yet another mistyped beginning. 'Who said anything about leaving home? I'm talking of theatreland, Ma. Of joining the ranks of the immortals.'

'Hmmm,' muttered Mrs Pond. 'Sweet are the days when nobody knows you, Lily. Who wants to be immortal? Immortality's a killer.'

'I doubt if *Love and Mr Holliday* is going to make me immortal, Ma. I doubt if it will make me anything. Still, judge for yourself.'

And this was where the owner and bearer of the oversize yellow rain-garments discovered the fatal loss. For nowhere in her supermarket holdall could she find any trace of her precious manuscript, the manuscript which in her dreams was going to bring her such fame and fortune that she would be able to transport her widowed mother and much loved little Russian grandmother from the dismal back streets of Streatham to the sunshine of Elysium.

'Murder,' she cried as she realised it had gone. 'I must have left it at the maniac's!'

To which her mother gave a look, the sort of look that only mothers can give to daughters when they haven't the faintest notion of what their offspring are talking about.

By the time Miss Lily Pond had finished typing Mr Matthew Browne's correspondence, it was evening of the next day, and the maniac had had ample chance to read several times through the manuscript he had found lying on top of his grand piano. He was much enjoying this unexpected treasure trove, and was certainly not in the mood to be interrupted by his doorbell which suddenly rang at five past seven. So he ignored it.

It rang again.

'Go away,' he said.

But it didn't. It rang once more, longer and louder.

Matt sighed, removed his glasses, crossed to the door and opened it. And there, standing on his threshold was the apparition in yellow PVC, once more heavily waterlogged. But this time he could see the face and the face was smiling at him.

'Lovely weather for drips,' it said as it removed the large rainsoaked sou'wester. 'It's folks like us what risk our lives so we can bring you the silver harvest of the sea.'

Which remark Matt failed to take in because he was taken aback by the beautiful blonde hair which had cascaded from her hat and which he observed was now swinging in two banana shaped bunches either side of a very pretty face.

'Mmmm?' he said, staring.

'Your letters.'

'What about my letters?' asked Matt, still unable to break the stare.

'Your *letters*,' said the bunches, proffering a large folder. 'I was here yesterday – remember? You were under a table.'

'I wasn't under a table,' said Matt, trying to close the door over and exclude this dangerous presence. 'Not really.'

'Yes you were,' the bunches persisted. 'That one.'

And with this she pushed the door back open and pointed at the dress table.

'I was?' asked Matt, cornered.

'Yes.'

'Yes. I was. That's right, I'd dropped a spoon. Thank you.'

Matt took the folder and attempted to shut the door once more, but Bunches foiled it by putting a well galoshed foot in it.

'Sorry. Strictly C.O.D.'

'What's strictly C.O.D.?'

'Cash on delivery the letters,' said Bunches. 'That's what. Four greenbacks and aren't you going to read them?'

Matt attempted once more to haul up the drawbridge, but the galosh was firmly wedged.

'I know what I wrote, thank you.'

'You don't know what I typed.'

She smiled at him and at last he managed to break his stare in order to glance briefly into the depths of the folder, a glance that could tell him nothing.

'Yes,' he muttered, 'they're fine thank you.'

And he pushed hard at the door.

'You're forgetting our friend the cod,' said Bunches in a funny voice. 'See hoo hoo dee.'

'See hoo hoo dee?' asked Matt, lost.

'The bunce, brother.'

Matt was now well and truly trapped, for his money was in his coat which was on the sofa and in order to get it he would have to leave the door unattended. But it was quite obvious that Bunches Galore had no intention of departing until this impending financial transaction had been made. So he darted back into his flat and searched his jacket for his purse.

'I should read them, if I were you,' called the voice from the door. 'If you value your freedom.'

'I'm sorry?' Matt called back.

'I said if I were you I'd look over the letters. The last person I did some typing for ended up in court because I kept leaving all the negatives out of his correspondence.'

Matt found his purse and turned around only to find to his horror Bunches Galore standing right beside him.

'Honestly. You'd be best to read them.'

Matt fumbled at the folder, deciding that the best tactic was to obey her instructions in the hope she would leave immediately he had carried them out. He pretended to check through the letters.

'Yes, yes,' he said, eyeing her. 'They're fine. Yes, they're fine.'

She smiled at him, a pleased smile. Then something caught his eye.

'Except – '

'Yes?'

'Except I don't know anybody called Mr Elephant. It's Oliphant.'

She moved closer and looked over his shoulder.

'And bill here – ' he continued, getting cross and waving a letter under her nose, 'bill here should have a small b, not a capital. This is meant to read "I have just received your present bill", not "I have just received your present, Bill." And what is THIS? What happened here?'

Bunches Galore took the letter and stared at it.

'Oh môche. I thought I'd got that out. I'm afraid that was Jacky. My mynah bird.'

And she handed him back the letter.

Matt took it and also stared at the distressing blot.

'What is it?' he enquired tentatively.

'Oh it's all right,' said Bunches, suddenly staring right into his eyes. 'It's not kack.'

She smiled reassuringly.

'He just has this nasty habit of spitting grapes at you from his cage. It'll come out. Are the rest okay?'

'No,' said Matt, handing her back the folder, 'You had better do them all again.'

Bunches took the letters and regarded them with deep sadness.

'Oh môche,' she said. 'I did so want them to be all nice for you.'

Matt was nearly caught completely off balance, but recovered sufficiently to strike home his advantage.

'Well – they're *not*,' he said, as firmly as he could. 'Now if you don't mind, I have some reading to do.'

And with that he picked up a manuscript and crossed to the sofa.

'Thank you,' he said terminally as he opened the cover and settled down to read.

'You can't read that!' cried Bunches, still hovering behind him. 'What are you reading that for?'

He looked up at her over his glasses.

'Because somebody left it behind. That dreadful – *thing* who was here yesterday. Never again. Never again will I attempt to work with a *woman*.'

Then he started to re-read.

'She didn't leave it behind,' said a very quiet voice, tentatively. 'I did.'

Matt looked at her slowly once more.

'What did you say?'

'Nothing.'

'How could you leave it behind?'

'By forgetting to take it with me?'

Matt held up the play.

'This is yours?'

'Yes,' replied Bunches.

Matt was now very confused. This couldn't be *her* play. Then the penny dropped.

'Of course,' he said. 'You typed it out.'

'Of course I typed it out,' said Bunches with complete honesty.

'Then you'll know who it's by,' said Matt, suddenly excited. 'For some reason there's no name on it.'

'The author's very modest,' said Bunches shyly.

'I've been looking for something like this to turn into a stage musical,' Matt continued, ignoring her. 'And this – this play – is *very* good.'

He removed his glasses and stared at her.

It was now Bunches's turn to be phased.

'No it isn't,' she said.

'We don't need your opinion. Just the name of the author. Who is he?'

'What's wrong with she?'

Matt slapped the manuscript in exasperation.

'No woman could have written this! This is not how women write! Just tell me his name.'

And with that he wandered over to the piano flicking through the pages of the play.

Lily looked desperately round the room for inspiration. A name. A Name. *Anything* would do. Anything rather than her own. Her gaze alighted on a bottle of Scotch.

'Scott Bottle,' she said.

Matt looked up at her, puzzled.

'*Botel*,' she corrected. 'Yes. Scott Botel.'

'You know him?'

'Sort of. I do his typing.'

'Fine. Then tell your friend Mr Botel I want to meet him,' Matt said and sat at his piano.

'You don't,' said Bunches.

'I do.'

'But – '

'No buts. Right?'

'No – '

But any further prevarication was useless, for the Maestro had started to play the 'Moonlight' Sonata in an obvious attempt to forestall further discussion. Lily found her feet still stuck to the floor.

Matt looked up at her finally from the piano.

'I said right.'

'Oh,' said Lily. 'Right.'

And with that she pulled a small face and crept to the door. She gave one last look to the man at the keyboard, but he had already shut her out. So she picked up her bag and left.

Matt watched the door close and stared after her. Women, he thought. Women. Then he heard something very odd and distinctly disturbing. For what he had started to play on the piano was no longer what he heard filling the room. He looked down at his hands. He had started out to play Beethoven, but he found to his bewilderment that he was now playing 'Blue Moon'.

As Lily padlocked her precious bicycle to the railing outside her temporary employer's flat, she half wondered how long she could keep this deception up. It was now three weeks since Mr Browne's initial interest in the mythical Scott Botel and, despite repeated postal exhortations from Mr Browne to Mr Botel for an urgent meeting to be arranged, Lily had so far managed to avoid the inevitable denouement, by the simple expedient of addressing all Mr Botel's mail from Mr Browne to her own address in Streatham and then replying as the playwright with a series of convoluted excuses as to why a meeting was not yet possible. So far so good, she thought as she pressed Mr Browne's doorbell. But sooner or later he was bound to discover the duplicity. Unless, of course, he lost interest in the play altogether; a faint hope which vanished from her mind completely as soon as she saw the intensely eager face that opened the door.

'Well?' it enquired, as Lily smiled at it and entered the inner sanctum.

'Sorry?'

'Well have you any news?'

'I've done your typing,' she said quickly, hoping to blind her opponent with speed. 'This week's mammoth bunch.'

She waved her carrier bag at him and then put it on the piano.

'Take that bag off my piano!'

'And it's getting better. Only thirteen erasions and four complete write-offs. See what you think.'

'Will you please take your bag off my piano?' demanded Matt once more, staring at the apparition now busily rummaging through her holdall. The girl phased him completely. The way she just marched into his flat! And scattered her belongings everywhere! And goodness knows what she thinks she looks like today with her trousers tucked into those ridiculous striped socks and that extraordinary cotton beach hat on that extraordinary head. He absent mindedly took the folder of letters she was waggling in front of him and flicked through them.

'You don't really earn a *living* like this, do you?' he asked.

'In one word,' she replied, 'you must be joking.'

'So what do you do normally?'

She shrugged.

'Nothing. Nothing much. I just boop around,' she said, picking up the fresh pile of letters from the table and beginning to read through them. 'Here and there. You know. Boop boop. Uh, uh.'

Lily stopped reading. The very first letter on the pile was to Mr Botel.

'Something wrong?' enquired her temporary employer.

'Not another Scott Botel letter?' she essayed lightheartedly. 'I mean – '

'Read it, please. We'll speak about its implications later.'

Lily looked at him and pulled a face.

'Read it, please' he reordered.

'Dear Mr Botel,' she began. 'Further to our prolonged correspondence and in anticipation of our mating – '

Matt snatched the letter and glared at her angrily.

'Let me see that,' he said, putting on his glasses and perusing the letter. 'Further to our prolonged correspondence and in anticipation of our *meeting* – '

He cleared his throat and flashed her what he hoped was a crisp glance. Lily smiled weakly. Then he continued reading.

'I would like to thank you for all the work you have done on your play following my recommendations.'

He stopped and peered at Lily over his spectacles.

'He's been very good, you know. He's taken all my advice.'

'Really?' she replied, all innocence. 'What an excellent pupil.'

'However,' Matt continued, returning to his letter, ' "I really must insist that we get together soon to discuss this project further. I am very impressed with your work, and I look forward to meeting you face to face." '

He looked up and found himself staring once more into Lily's face.

He cleared his throat.

'Yours sincerely,' he said.

'Matthew Brown,' said she.

'With an e.'

'With an e.'

There was a silence, with neither of them quite able to break the hold. Lily got off first.

'Right,' she said briskly. 'Now I really must boop off.'

'No. No, no don't go – booping off. I want to ask you something.'

'I really can't stay.'

'It really won't take long, Miss – er – . . . Look.'

Matt picked up her – correction, Scott Botel's – manuscript and waved it at her.

'Look. This man – your friend. What are we going to do about him?'

This was the moment Lily had dreaded. It was obviously all going to come to a head this very moment.

'We?' she squeaked. 'Sorry – *we*?'

'Yes,' replied Matt irritably. 'We. Why *won't* your Mr Botel meet me?'

'He's a very busy man, Mr Browne.'

Lily tried edging towards the door but Matt quickly cut her off.

'I've written to him at least half a dozen times and all he does is prevaricate.'

'He's very good at that,' said Lily feebly.

'Surely he can meet me one evening?'

Lily looked at his eager and puzzled face hopelessly, then sank down on to the sofa.

'No.'

Matt sat down beside her.

'Of course he can.'

'He can't.'

'Why not?'

'Because,' Lily said, hoping desperately for inspiration. 'Because – he's a prisoner.'

Matt stared even harder at her.

'A *prisoner*?'

'Yes,' continued Lily, now getting into her stride. 'And he's not allowed out. In fact I'm the only person he's allowed to see because he's – incredibly dangerous.'

In the ensuing stunned silence, she risked a furtive peek at Matt's face to see how she was doing so far. She surmised from the deep furrows on his forehead that the story so far was so far so good.

Matt nodded.

'I see. And what's he inside for?'

Lily wasn't quite ready for this one.

'Er – being incredibly dangerous.'

'But what did he *do* that he went inside for?'

He was staring at her awfully hard.

'Yes,' she muttered pathetically and then lapsed into silence. 'G.B.S.'

Matt's furrows got even deeper.

'G.B.*S.*?'

'Yes,' said Lily, now well and truly trapped. 'You know. Grievous bodily . . . shoplifting?'

Matt got up from the sofa in total exasperation and walked over to the window.

'Look – Miss . . . I have the feeling,' he said, addressing the street below, 'that you are covering up for somebody. I mean – Scott Botel. That just has to be a nom de plume.'

'No,' said Lily helpfully. 'It's just something he writes under. Under which he – '

'Will you stop wasting time!' roared Matt, 'Sorry. It's just that I have a feeling you are not telling me the truth. Right?'

'Wrong,' Lily smiled. 'I'm just lying.'

'Ah. Then Mr Scott Botel does not exist.'

Matt smiled triumphantly. Lily smiled back.

'Yes he does. He makes a lot of people very happy.'

'Just tell me the truth!' roared Matt again, trying to control the rising cadences of his speech. 'Who is the author of this play?'

It was all over. Oh well – here goes.

'I am,' she admitted.

'WILL YOU STOP PLAYING GAMES? WHO WROTE THIS PLAY?' he thundered.

Isn't it typical? thought Lily. You tell people the truth and all they do is get belligerent. So. So what was she meant to do now? He wanted to know the author and now he knew the author he didn't want to know the author.

'Who wrote this *PLAY*?'

She looked to the window in the faint hope that she might be able to overpower him and make a daring escape down the fire escape, but unhappily it wasn't that sort of window. But she did catch sight of a builder's sign hanging directly opposite which told her who wrote the play.

'For the very last time, Miss er – ' Matt demanded, taking the volume down several decibels. 'Who – wrote – this – play?'

Lily quickly checked with the sign once more then replied:

'Lionel Blanchard,' – fortunately omitting the 'And Sons Ltd'.

'Ah!' said her inquisitor, well pleased. 'And *who* is Lionel Blanchard?'

'The author of the play,' she replied, shaking her head. Ask a silly question . . .

Matt stared at her tightly.

'What does Lionel Blanchard do?'

Lily smiled hopefully.

'Writes plays?'

Matt breathed in very slowly in an intense effort to control his always all-too-easily-lost patience.

'We know Lionel Blanchard writes plays,' he agreed, slowly and calmly, 'But what does Lionel Blanchard do that makes Lionel Blanchard so busy that I cannot meet Lionel Blanchard?'

'He works nights,' muttered Lily from the depths of the trap.

'Then I will meet him during the *day*,' continued Matt remorselessly.

'He'll be asleep,' said Lily, hearing the door closing fast.

'Then I will wake him up!'

Matt turned to her triumphantly and hit her manuscript with the palm of his hand.

'I have to meet this man! This man has the sort of mind I *like*.'

Lily frowned.

'He has?'

'Yes. Yes – so – fix up a meeting. Any day. Any time. But this week. And then let me know. I am getting tired of being fobbed off.'

Lily bit her lip. Perhaps she should try to explain again once and for all. But her inquisitor was waving her carrier bag under her nose, obviously anxious to draw stumps on the day's play.

'Is that understood?' he asked as she got up and started to edge for the door.

'Understood,' she answered faintly, turning the Yale lock open.

'And you have forgotten your shoes!'

She turned round to find him glaring at her and holding out the pair of shoes she had nervously scuffed off under the coffee table during the Lionel Blanchard revelations.

'Thank you,' she said and smiled at him as she put them on.

He turned away from her and held open the door.

'Do you know something?'

'What?' he asked gruffly, turning back to her.

She grinned at him.

'You'd have made an awfully good Brown Owl.'

Lily took fresh stock of the situation while her mother diligently brushed out the golden tresses of her hair and sighed. Unfortunately the regular strokes of the hairbrush were not having their normal therapeutic effect. Ever since she could remember, her mother had always sat her down whenever she was upset or brokenhearted, or half strangled by an attack of the mean reds, and brushed her hair, to such great effect that after about half an hour Lily's particular malaise of the moment had either disappeared completely or been drastically cut down to size. But this evening it wasn't working and in her heart she knew the real reason was that this time she was no longer waving, but desperately near to drowning.

All right, she thought, all right – she'd got herself into this particular mess so she'd have to get herself out. But never for one moment had she thought that Oberfuhrer Browne would pursue so remorselessly his quest to meet the mythical Lionel Blanchard. Of course she could have simply stopped going to his flat. She could have told them at the agency that he was making a nuisance of himself and asked to be assigned to a more salubrious job. Salubrious? Well anyway – she could easily have detached herself from him and bicycled swiftly out of reach and out of his life. But that would have meant she wouldn't see him again – and it would have meant . . . Lily wasn't altogether sure of what else it would have meant, because one thing she did know for certain was that she didn't know what anything meant any more.

She looked at her watch and more panic set in.

'I'm going to be late, Ma!' she said, getting to her feet and tucking her tee shirt back into her jeans.

'Lily.'

Her mother spread her hands out and gave her that look.

'And you think brushing your hair's good enough?'

'Ma.' Lily turned and looked at her mother. 'The way he feels about women it wouldn't matter if I turned up completely leafless.'

'So do you know how he feels about pretty girls?'

Lily went to her wardrobe and took down her wind-cheater.

'I'm only going to fess up to him, Ma. Tell him the whole sordid and squalid truth about L. Blanchard, Esq. – not give him the Ritzi Mitzi.'

'Mmm,' shrugged her mother. 'Whenever you have to tell the truth to a man, Lily, is exactly when you *should* be giving him the Ritzi Mitzi.'

Lily made for the door, but her mother barred the way.

'You are not going out dressed like that, Lily. Just for once you'll do as I say and put on a dress. Something – suitable.'

'I haven't *got* a dress, Ma. At least not a something – suitable dress.'

But Mrs Pond now had the wind under her tail and was half-way down the corridor before Lily could stop her.

'I know just the thing!' she called.

'Oh really?' Lily shouted after her. 'Well whatever it is it had better be rocketproof.'

If Lily Pond was in a state that evening, there is no way of describing the condition of the vigilant Matthew Browne. He had already had an incident with the drink cupboard, the sort of experience very few men of maturity enjoy as a curtain raiser to an important evening. Finding himself in a hypertense state he had sought some comfort in a glass of single malt, only to find his decanter empty. Luckily he always kept his cellar well stocked, so he had opened a fresh bottle and decanted it. But before he could pour himself a drink, the phone rang, and in his anguished condition he replaced the empty bottle in the cupboard and dropped the full decanter into the waste paper basket where it spilled its precious contents through the wicker work on to the floor. He had put this unusually anxious state of his down to his excitement at the prospect of meeting Lionel Blanchard, but something somewhere deep inside him told him this was not the case. That it was the prospect of seeing again someone so different from anybody else he had seen that was causing him these infuriatingly palpitating moments.

The doorbell rang – once, sharply, and Matt spilt his whisky up his sleeve.

It rang again and he found himself running to answer it. He stopped and collected himself in time. Then he took a deep breath, shook the whisky from his sleeve and put on his best frown.

And opened the door.

Fortunately, or unfortunately, depending how you view it, life has a way of forever upsetting the most well composed of apple-carts and as Matt opened the door you could hear the sound of tumbling pippins for miles around. In his mind's eye he had been expecting Lily, but the vision that stood before him in the hall was not the Lily he had seen and stored away in his memory. This was a Lily he had never seen, in a long cream dress with her hair beautifully done.

This was an apparition of the most sublime delight. Not that the Lily he had seen before was not nice, he hastened to add to himself. The Lily he was used to seeing was a confection of the highest order, but confections are confections, while apparitions are – well – apparitions are something else.

'Oh. It's you.'

He walked back into the heart of the flat.

'Aren't you good?' said Lily, following. 'Recognising me. Sorry if I'm a bit late.'

'A *bit* late?' exclaimed Matt, exposing a chink in the armour. 'You're not late,' he added hurriedly, 'but we will be if we don't get going. We don't want to keep Mr Blanchard waiting any longer. Particularly since he's giving up a bit of his valuable evening.'

Matt closed over the drink cupboard and looked around for his keys.

Lily shifted anxiously from one leg to another, like a flamingo newly arrived at the zoo.

'No,' she said, 'But don't you think you ought to have a drink first? People in films always have a drink when they've just received bad news.'

'Bad news?' said Matt. 'I haven't received any bad news.'

'Yet,' replied Lily.

Matt looked at her crossly.

'So what's the bad news – you haven't got married or something stupid have you?'

She looked at him suddenly, right in the eyes. Matt fidgeted in anguish, pre-empted by his own tongue.

'I mean,' he muttered, 'I mean – simply because – the state of marriage is – a state. It gets everybody in a state.'

He rushed past her to get to the door.

'Shall we go?'

Lily stood quite still for a moment, still phased by his chance question. Then she got there.

'Oh – the dress!'

She turned to him, waiting.

'The *dress*. You thought I'd – ? This is just my little grannie's old wedding dress. And my mother's funny old idea.'

She smiled reassuringly at him, which was returned by a blank look. They crossed the hall to the lift.

'There's some good news as well by the way,' Lily added

by way of distraction as they waited for the car.

'It's like that old joke. There's good news and there's bad news. Which would you like first?'

'I only enjoy bad news,' Matt replied. 'It makes me feel in less of a minority.'

And with that the lift arrived.

Matt held open the door for her.

'Then I'll tell you the bad news first,' Lily said as Matt bustled her into the cage.

'You – are going to meet Lionel Blanchard.'

'I know that,' said Matt. 'Come *on*.'

'And now for the bad news.'

Matt pressed the button.

'Yes, yes, yes.'

Lily pulled a small face as the doors closed over.

'You're not going to like it.'

The lift doors reopened after a not very long interval. It had taken Lily precisely the time it had taken the lift to travel to the ground floor to impart to Matt the bad news. Whereupon he straightaway reprogrammed the lift to return to the fourth floor.

'I told you you weren't going to like it,' mumbled Lily as Matt crossed briskly to the flat door.

'I told you.'

But Matt had already unlocked the door and let himself in. By the time Lily eased herself warily round the still-open door he was already pouring for himself what looked like to her nine fingers of whisky. She edged further into the room and stood sparely clutching her carrier bag, waiting for her inevitable annihilation.

Matt sat suddenly on the edge of his sofa and started to play in some desperation with his executive toy – a pacifier made of steel balls suspended on string. Lily watched the infuriatingly clicking spheres.

'I bet you feel like getting under a table,' she ventured.

Lily removed one of her shoes with her other and stood flamingo-like scratching the back of her leg with her now bare foot.

'I certainly feel like getting under a table.'

Silence. Matt got up and walked over to the window. More silence.

'Well then,' tried Lily, only to be greeted with even stonier silence.

'Well then.'

Matt stared into his empty glass and swirled the melting orbs of ice. There was no point in delaying this meeting any longer.

'So what are you hanging about for?' he demanded, still resolutely staring into his glass, rather than risking a look at her.

'We've got an early start in the morning.'

He heard a sharp little intake of breath from behind him.

'We?' squeaked Lily, aghast. 'We?'

'Yes,' replied Matt. 'We.'

'Oh I say,' gasped Lily, hugging her carrier bag to her chest. '*We*. Oh I *say*.'

And she tumbled out of the room, leaving behind in the middle of the floor one flat evening sandal.

After a moment, Matt turned to see where she had been standing and saw the place landmarked by her discarded shoe. He picked it up and for the first time for a long time Matthew Browne really smiled.

CHAPTER TWO

Overtures and Beginners

Early starts were something at which Lily had never exactly excelled. Here she was at ten to nine the following morning, having twice been right through the entire contents of her not very vast wardrobe yet still without even the vaguest of ideas as to what was the correct 'costume de combat'. She sat on her bed, pulled her knees up under her chin and stared at her poster of Pele for inspiration.

Her mother pushed open the bedroom door with her back and came in carrying two mugs of coffee.

'Not dressed yet?' she said accusingly.

'No I'm not dressed yet, Ma, because I can't make up my mind what to wear. It makes it très difficult – what with him being allergic to women.'

Lily gave a little sigh.

'I feel just like I did before my cycling test.'

Her mother looked at her in near despair, then started to sort through the clothes in the wardrobe.

'Where's your gumption, Lily? You people nowadays are giving up all the time.'

She waved a pink gingham pinafore dress, which Lily had always loathed, in the air for emphasis.

'Let me tell you something. It certainly wasn't wearing rubber gloves for washing up that won the Battle of Britain.'

Thankfully the pinafore dress was returned to the cupboard.

'This man likes your play,' her mother continued. 'He said so.'

'He was probably being polite,' muttered Lily.

'Polite my elbow. From what you tell me this proxy

Beethoven makes Hitler sound like a housepainter.'

'Hitler *was* a housepainter, Ma.'

'Then he should have stuck to it. Better a busy housepainter than a dead dictator.'

Mrs Pond held up a red dress.

'What is wrong with this?'

'Nothing's *wrong* with that, Ma – '

'Then if there is nothing wrong with it – '

Her mother gave it a closer look.

'Mind you. If your composer can keep his composure with you wearing this, then there's something wrong with his stringing.'

Lily got off the bed and took the dress from her mother.

'Oh to hell. And anyway, Tom likes it.'

Her mother smiled.

'Yes. Yes, wear it for Tom. Didn't he buy it for your birthday?'

'He did,' said Lily, struggling into the dress. 'And didn't I have to lend him the money?'

'Poor Tom.'

'Tom's all right. Zip me up, Ma. I'd better get a wiggle on. I mustn't be late for work on the first *day*. And I've still got to pump up my back tyre.'

Lily picked up her carrier bag and took her cycling cape down off the back of the door.

'You should give up that bicycle, Lily. You'll get swimmer's legs.'

'How can I possibly get swimmer's legs from riding a bicycle?'

'You've seen these swimmer's legs? They look as if they go everywhere on a bicycle.'

Mrs Pond helped her daughter into her yellow cape then turned her round for the final appraisal.

'Let me look at you.'

'Please, Ma,' said Lily, tactfully disengaging herself. 'It's five to nine. The one thing I mustn't be is late.'

And she wouldn't have been, if certain ifs and ands had been the proverbial pots and pans. For while crossing Clapham Common her tired back tyre, already composed more of puncture repair pads than of virgin rubber, finally refused to hold any further air and expired gracelessly on the slope of a hill. *If* she had remembered to buy a new inner tube, and *if* she had carried her spare back wheel as advised by Our Man on The Road in *Cycle and Cyclist*, *and* if she carried her motorway emergency mending kit – she'd have made their deadline with time to spare. Ifs and ands. They were the bane of her existence. And furthermore, she was now going to be very late.

Of which fact Matt was fast becoming aware, as his grandfather clock chimed for the twelfth time that day. Obviously she wasn't just going to be late. She obviously wasn't coming at all.

He picked up the small bunch of red roses he had bought her and tossed them into the waste paper basket. Then he sat down at his piano and assassinated the 'Appassionata'.

Lily heard the sounds of his piano as traffic stained and rain sodden she tiptoed from the lift to his open flat door. He looked extremely cross, she thought, sitting hammering the keys with his glasses perched on his nose and a pencil stuck in his mouth.

She squeezed in, sotto, and made her quiet way to the piano.

'You're late,' said Matt, but not until he had finished playing.

'I got a flat in Clapham.'

'You said you lived in Streatham.'

'Flat tyre. Sur ma bicyclette. Sorry.'

Matt polished his glasses, still resolutely looking away from her.

'There is only one thing more useless than being late,' he announced. 'And that is being sorry for it.'

'Right,' replied Lily, suitably abashed. 'As my mother always says – it is vain to look for yesterday's fish in the house of the otter.'

Matt stared blankly at her.

'You were meant to be here over an hour and a half ago. Two hours ago in fact.'

'In fiction I'm afraid. I know. Sorry.'

Lily pulled off her cycling cape. It was an awkward garment at the best of times, and at the worst of times – namely when being discarded – was positively graceless. Once again she found herself trapped within its clammy confines as she struggled to escape, her arms stuck helplessly in the air while about her billowed yards of yellow oil-cloth.

'Sorry!' she shouted from within.

She bent over double and pointed herself at Matt.

'Do you think you could give a yank?'

Matt tugged at the garment and soon Lily was free. Once more he found himself staring at her.

'Sorry,' she said, diving into her carrier bag and producing a hair brush. 'I must look an awful mess.'

And she proceeded to brush out her blonde hair quickly and efficiently.

'Right.'

The brush had been returned to the carrier and she now stood looking at him expectantly. Matt cleared his throat.

'Right,' he replied. 'Would you like to sit down?'

'If you'd like me to. Where would you like me to sit?'

Matt waved his hands in what he hoped was a gracious and generous manner.

'Please. It's all the same to me.'

'Really? Well where do *you* like to sit?'

'I don't,' said Matt. 'I stand. You can sit.'

'But it's not really fair me sitting down,' protested Lily. 'Not if you're standing.'

'Very well then. Stand.'

'But I'll sit if you really want me to.'

'Sit,' said Matt, beginning to lose patience. 'Stand. It's all the same to me but for God's sake SIT DOWN!'

Lily, caught by the sudden change in mood, was immediately seated.

'That's *my* chair!'

She stood up again. Matt pointed to the sofa.

'Over there. Now then.'

Lily sat nervously on the edge of the sofa and rummaged in her carrier.

'My mother thinks you should avoid sitting whenever possible.'

She produced a pencil and smiled up at Matt.

'She says it gives you British Botty. Right.'

Matt stared at the apparition smiling so eagerly at him from his sofa, but there was still a little ice in his heart. She may be beautiful, but she was female and so far nothing that had happened this morning allayed the fear he nursed about working with a member of the opposite sex. He picked up her manuscript which he had re-read again the night before and tapped it thoughtfully.

'This play of yours.'

'Yes?' Lily leant forward in anticipation of his mighty judgement.

Matt found he had forgotten what he was going to say.

'You were saying?'

'I was?'

'Yes. This play of mine.'

'Ah.'

He had not realised defeat would stare him in the face so soon. So he sat in his chair and covering his face with his hands gave a low moan.

Lily, thinking she was missing the keenly anticipated Great Words, leaned even further forward.

Matt, opening his fingers slightly in front of his eyes, accidentally caught a glimpse of the sight from which he was hiding. He closed his fingers over and uttered another moan.

'Are you all right?'

'No.'

'What's wrong?'

'What is wrong. What is wrong is that I cannot work with you – like this.'

'Can't you?' Lily asked, somewhat fearfully.

'No I can't,' replied the non-seeing Matt. 'So we must sort things out. You see, I have never successfully co-operated with a woman. Professionally that is. I mean I only agreed to work with you because I thought you were a man which you are quite obviously not. And I am. Naturally, I'd rather you weren't. A woman – purely for the purposes of our work. Right? Right. Because I accepted your work – in the belief – that you were a writer – called Lionel Blanchard. Because that was the name you chose to write under.'

'Under which I chose to – '

Two fingers parted, and an angry eye glared out for a split second at Lily. Then they closed again. Lily fell silent.

'So as far as I'm concerned, you *are* Lionel Blanchard.'

'I am Lionel Blanchard.'

'You are Lionel Blanchard.'

Lily sat back and gave it some thought. The man behind the hands gave a deep sigh and was silent.

'Yes, perhaps it would help me, too,' said Lily. 'You see

I've never worked with anyone before either. Except my mother. Perhaps *I* should look upon *you* as my mother.'

The fingers parted again and the dark eyes flashed. Lily was less scared. In time you can get used to anything.

'And I can't possibly work with you in that dress.'

'Point,' Lily agreed. 'Hardly the sort of ensemble Lionel Blanchard would sport. Unless he was a trifle acey deucey. I'll take it off.'

'No you won't.'

'Yes I will. I mustn't put you off your stroke. 'Smatter-offact, I always work in my dressing gown at home. Have you a dressing gown?'

'I have a dressing gown. It's behind my bedroom door.'

'May I borrow it?'

'You may borrow it.'

'Ta.'

'And then perhaps we can get on.'

'I'll drink to that.'

Matt removed his hands from his eyes to discover the red dress beating a hasty retreat to his bedroom.

'If it wasn't for Tom,' it said, 'I wouldn't have put this on at all.'

Beautifully timed, thought Matt as he watched the bedroom door. Superb. The little stone dropped in the centre of the puddle which was guaranteed to send ripples right out to the very edges.

'Tom?' he found himself asking. 'Who's Tom?'

He knew what the reply would be. It was standard. Nobody.

'Nobody,' came the standard reply from the bedroom.

And in standard response, Matt got up and poured himself a drink.

'Tom's, well – . . . oh rot this zip.'

'Don't bother,' Matt called. 'I'm not interested.'

'Sorry?'

'I said "Don't bother".'

Lily put her head round the door.

'But I've taken my dress off now.'

'I meant about Tom.'

'Tom?'

'Don't bother. I'm not interested.'

Lily frowned and closed the door. What a strange man, she

thought as she wrapped the short silk dressing gown about her. Why should he be interested in Tom? He really was a very strange man altogether.

When she re-entered the sitting room, demurely attired in the composer's knee length patterned silk dressing gown that on her reckoning could easily pass for one of the season's latest coat dresses, she found him standing in the corner by the grandfather clock feeling the glands in his neck.

'Are you okay?' she asked him.

'I am fine,' he answered, albeit a mite croakily. 'Fine.'

'You don't look it. You look a little peaky.'

He was immediately concerned.

'I do?'

Lily took his wrist.

'And your pulse is fast.'

'It is?'

He took his wrist away from her and checked his pulse, while Lily peered closely at his chest.

'*And* you've got some egg on your jumper.'

'I have?'

She looked at him seriously.

'High colour, racing pulse, egg on jumper. You ate your breakfast too fast.'

Matt wiped his by now slightly clammy forehead and picked up the typescript.

'I'm sure I'll live,' he said, hopeful that the sardonic tone of his voice would inform his pupil that he was in no mood for jokes.

'And now perhaps we can get on.'

Duly crushed, Lily was about to comply when the grandfather clock chimed half past twelve in her ear and she was unfortunately reminded of another more pressing engagement.

'I'd love to – ' she said hesitantly.

'Love to what?'

He was looking at her again.

'Love to – get on. You know. But I can't.'

She edged back towards the bedroom door.

'Why can't you?'

'Because I have to go.'

She blocked her mental ears, waiting for the holocaust. Instead she was aware only of a low hissing sound.

'May I remind you,' he seethed, 'that you have only just *got* here?'

'I don't need reminding,' Lily backed off as fast as she could. 'Blush blush.'

She tapped the clock beside her.

'I mean look at the time. He'll be here any moment.'

She made for the bedroom door but found Matt there before her.

'*Who* will be here any moment?'

'Nobody,' she evaded, ducking neatly under his outstretched arm and reaching the safety of the bedroom. 'The person you don't want to know about.'

She shut the door, then re-opening it, peered briefly out at him.

'The person *about* whom – '

The look on Matt's face advised her to re-shut the door. She did so, swiftly. He reopened it.

'Tim?'

'Tom.'

This time she engaged the lock, then leant against the door, movie style, to draw a welcome breath. Only one problem, she hadn't got her frock.

'Môche,' she muttered.

She could hardly go back out there. He might be the sort of person who became violent when roused. Every composer she'd ever seen on the silver screen had always been prone to turbulence. They were forever dashing themselves suicidally into raging torrents or beating up their beloveds with rejected symphonies. She peered cautiously through the keyhole and, sure enough, there he was, hurling slub silk sofa cushions at the flocked wallpaper.

She opened the door a fraction.

'Excuse me?'

The demented cushion hurler whipped round, mid-throw.

'Now what?'

'It's my dress. I left it out there. Could you pass it through please?'

But he made no move. He just stood his ground and stared wildly at her. Lily could have sworn she could see steam coming out of his ears. She re-barred the door.

Matt, however, was not contemplating further acts of violence. Instead, an interesting thought had entered his head, namely no dress, no exit. He was damned to see why she should go waltzing off to lunch with her lover when they were meant to be starting work together.

'Your dress?' he called, as casually as he could.

'Yes,' came a voice from the bedroom. 'It's in my carrier.'

He could see it, lying neatly folded on top of the bag on the sofa.

'Where did you say it was?' he enquired, carefully taking it out and tucking it behind his back.

'In my carrier. Listen. I'd better explain about Tom. Just in case you get the wrong end of the whatever.'

'In your *carrier*?' Matt called, overacting as always.

'Yes. You see – Tom – who's a doctor. At St George's actually. Just round the corner. It's his birthday you see – '

'Oh yes?' said Matt, tip-toeing to the piano and carefully hiding the dress under the lid. 'Well, it's not in your bag now.'

Lily put her head round the door.

'It must be.'

'It isn't.'

The front door bell rang.

'And that could be Tom.'

'I'll see to him,' volunteered Matt, suddenly as nice as spring sunshine. 'Don't worry, I'll soon see to him.'

As he sauntered to the door, Lily, clad only in her peach camisole, stole to the sofa, grabbed her carrier and fled back to the bedroom, locking the door behind her.

Matt opened his front door and to his deep dismay was greeted by an extremely handsome and sunny countenanced young man.

'Her – her – hello,' stammered the young man nervously.

'Hello,' answered Matt coldly.

'Is Ler-Lily here please?'

'She is, yes, but I'm afraid she's not ready. In fact she's not even dressed.'

Matt smiled, pleased with his now famed brutality.

'Not der-der-dressed?'

Matt smiled even more broadly. His ploy was having its required effect.

'No. She is still as yet – unclad.'

'Good Ler-Lord. But she ser-ser-said half p-past.'

'She did?'

'Yer-yes.'

The young man peered into the flat.

'She is her-here?'

'She certainly is,' said Matt lightly. 'She most certainly is. And shall I tell you where she is precisely? She is in my bedroom. Looking for her dress.'

The young man coloured even more deeply.

'Ger-ger-gracious.'

'Gracious is understating it. I'll tell her you called.'

Matt shut the door over slightly, barring the young man any access.

'That's er-frightfully kind. And would you also ter-tell her I'll wait for her round the cer-corner in San D-Dominico's? Ther-thanks.'

With which he backed off quickly to the lift and Matt closed the door triumphantly. Then he turned to find Lily back in his dressing gown, searching the room for her dress.

'Was that Tom?' she asked nervously.

'No,' said Matt flatly. 'Tom who?'

'Who was it then?'

'Personal. It was personal.'

Lily lifted up the cushions on the sofa and peered hopelessly under them. The clock chimed another quarter.

'Môche. I'd better go and wait for him in the restaurant then. Then I won't be so late back.'

Matt frowned at this piece of logic then watched bemusedly as she picked up her carrier bag and looked hopelessly inside for the last time. No dress, no exit.

'You can hardly go out to lunch without your dress.'

Which gave Lily pause for thought. What was wrong with the way she was? Perhaps he'd object.

'Would you mind?' she asked him.

'Mind what?'

'If I went out in this?'

She held up the hem of the dressing gown to signal her intention.

'You can't go out in that!'

'Why not? It's perfectly respectable. Nobody'll even notice.'

For the second time that morning Lily could swear she saw not only steam escaping from the maestro's ears but possibly flames as well.

'Of *course* they'll notice! Nobody goes out to lunch in their *dressing* gown!'

Lily shrugged.

'Think of it as a coat dress. As a matter of fact, I think it's pretty snappy.'

She made her move to the door. Matt tried one last desperate interruption.

'Lionel,' he appealed.

'Don't worry,' she replied. 'I'll be as quick as I can, Mother.'

And with a small smile, she was gone.

Matt picked up a cushion and hurled it at the sofa. Then he picked up the red roses he had earlier rescued from the waste paper basket and threw them back among the refuse.

'Women!'

Lily's lunch date with Tom was proceeding quite smoothly with not even her dining partner having commented on her attire when they were interrupted by the head waiter busily being urgento.

'Scuse, Signorina,' he apologised, 'But signor. Your ospital on the phone. E say you moss come bick quick. Ees urgento. Mose urgento.'

Tom sighed and pushed his chair back.

'Ser-sorry, Lily.'

'I'm sorry for you, Tom,' answered Lily. 'On your birthday.'

'I know,' said Tom. 'It's the first time it's ever happened to me.'

It was also the first time Matthew Browne had employed such underhand tactics to disrupt another party's social arrangements, and as he sat back in his armchair trying to clear an ominously fevering head, he wondered what particular devil had possessed him. Why should he want her back now? Half past two would have been perfectly acceptable.

He sneezed.

'Blast!'

Because he was a professional – that's why he had wanted her back. That's why he'd telephoned the restaurant to send Tom, Tom the Piper's Son off on a wild goose chase. Purely for professional reasons. They had to be utterly professional together in this new relationship-partnership. He rescued the roses once more from the refuse and dusted them off. His doorbell rang.

He sneezed again.

'Blast!'

It was going to be a cracker, he thought as he made his way to the door. The sort of cold you could almost really enjoy.

Lily gave him a brief smile as he admitted her.

'Short lunch.'

'He was called back to the hospital.'

Matt made the appropriate clucking noises.

'Lives before lasagne and all that jive,' Lily continued as she made her way to the sofa.

'Oh dear dear dear,' over-sympathised Matt. 'Called back to the hospital? Oh dear dear dear.'

Lily looked at him suspiciously. Like all bad actors he was busy making his presence unduly felt. Then another sight distracted her. Her red dress, neatly folded on the back of the armchair.

'You found my dress then. Where was it?'

Matt was wrong footed before he even knew it.

'Where I'd hidden it,' he confessed.

'*Hidden* it?'

'Sorry,' Matt sneezed. 'Sorry. I mean where I found it hidden. In the – under the piano. It must have got in under the piano and hidden itself and – blast!'

Another sneeze. Lily's look of anger now changed to one of concern. She was a born mother hen.

'You're ill, aren't you?'

Matt looked suitably doleful, never being one to let a good opportunity pass by.

'I think the egg on my jumper has turned into something nasty on my chest.'

He'd got her. She was now looking positively Doctor Kildare-ish.

'You do appear a little pasty.'

'I always appear a little pasty.'

'You should be in bed.'

Matt sneezed again and added a couple of convincing shivers.

'Yes, you really should be in bed. You go to bed and give me a ring when you're better.'

'There never is a time when I'm *better*,' Matt complained. 'There are merely times when I'm less ill.'

She turned him gently but decisively towards the bedroom.

'I'll bring you in a hot whisky and honey and Disprin.'

Whoever said the way to a man's heart was through his stomach got it all wrong, Matt thought. The way to his affection was straight through his hypochondria.

He surreptitiously picked up the bunch of roses and hid them behind his back.

'Lionel,' said Matt. 'Lionel.'

'Yes?' said Lily.

'Lionel.'

He thrust the roses at her, not at all like he had planned to do.

'For you.'

And he rushed into the bedroom, nearly braining himself on the doorpost.

Lily looked at the flowers. He was semi-human after all.

'Matt?'

No reply. She called out more loudly.

'Matt? Thanks.'

She looked again at the flowers. What had he bought her flowers for? He mysoginised for the world, surely? What on earth had he bought her flowers for?

'Sorry for mucking up the morning,' she called. 'I didn't really say sorry for mucking up the morning!'

There was a sort of grunt from within, then more silence.

The phone rang.

'Shall I get it?' Lily volunteered.

Matt was half in and half out of his pyjamas and in no fit state to speak to anybody anyway.

'Yes,' he called.

Lily answered the phone.

'Hello? Matthew Browne's drum? Who?'

It was Tom.

'It's all right!' she called. 'It's only Tom.'

All right? It was certainly not all right, thought Matt, as panic struck he tried to make sense of his fast tangling pyjamas. What was the interfering fool doing ringing up here?

Lily was listening with now darkening countenance to the

telephone as Matt staggered back into the sitting room. He picked up the drink she had started to prepare him and sipped it nervously. Tom couldn't possibly put the finger on him, Matt reasoned. There was no way he could have guessed. But from the expression on Lily's face as she replaced the receiver he knew that some game or other was up.

'Tom's call from the hospital was a funny ha-ha,' she said with that terrible calmness women get when deeply annoyed. 'A wild goose chase.'

'A wild choose gase?' croaked Matt. 'That's awful.'

'Isn't it?' she agreed. 'And there was only one clever Richard who knew we were eating at San Dominico's.'

'Nonsense,' Matt said. 'It was probably some drunk medic.'

'Some drunk medic my elbow.'

Lily gave him an extremely measured look.

'Some twisted composer much more likely.'

And with that she locked herself back in his bedroom.

'What are you doing?' Matt shouted through the keyhole.

In all his life he never expected to find himself shouting at a woman through a keyhole.

'I'm going back to finish my lunch with Tom!'

'Well you might at least let me have my dressing gown! I could catch my death of cold like this!'

The door opened briefly and his dressing gown was expelled viciously, wrapping itself around Matt's aching head.

'Thank you,' said Matt.

'My pleasure,' Lily answered, relocking the door and finding once more that she was without her all important top garment.

Matt slipped into his dressing gown and saw lying on his chair her all important garment.

'Excuse me?' a voice called from within.

'Yes?' Matt answered, neatly lobbing the dress on to the top of the drink cupboard.

'My dress.'

'I thought you had it.'

A furious blonde head appeared at the doorway.

'It's fun and games time again is it?'

'I don't know what you are talking about. I just wish you'd hurry up so that I could regain possession of my bedroom.'

He smiled, courteously. She gave him her filthiest of looks.

The bedroom door slammed and was locked.

Her mother was right. People needed to use their gumption. And now was the chance for her to use hers.

Matt was well on top of a little number by Scarlatti when the bedroom door was reopened, and Miss Pond reappeared. Matt stopped playing and stared. She looked magnificent, with her hair piled high, and clad in a full length pink striped dress with matching shoulder bag and then Matt got the message.

'That's one of my sheets! You can't go out to lunch in one of my sheets!'

'Try and stop me, Buster.'

'And what are you doing with my pillowcase? You can't go out to lunch in a sheet and pillow case!'

'Why not? Caesar ruled an empire in a frock.'

She emptied the contents of her brown paper carrier into the pillowcase, then made for the door.

'Now if you'll excuse me, I must go and finish my lunch.'

Matt started towards his bedroom.

'Really? Well I feel like having some lunch as well.'

'Dressed like that?' she asked coolly.

'I have a wardrobe full of clothes in there,' he answered, equally coolly.

'So you have.'

Matt guessed too late what she was planning and by the time he had reached the bedroom door she had it firmly locked and the key in her pillow bag.

'Get well soon,' she said and swept out.

Matt picked up the bunch of red roses and beat them to death on the back of his chair.

'We'll be quite safe now,' said Lily, deep in menu consultation. 'I've taken steps to prevent interruption.'

'He's got a pre-pretty warped sense of her-humour, that's all I can say,' concluded Tom.

'You're telling me. But I don't think we'll be bothered again.'

Lily put down the menu, just in time to see the Mad Matt appearing at the top of the restaurant steps in mackintosh and pyjamas.

'But I speak too soon,' said Lily.

'Ah. Signor Browne,' greased the head waiter. 'What a loving suprise.'

The Invalid ignored the welcome and giving vent to a resounding sneeze his face searched the restaurant for his victim.

'But you'ave not book, and see?'

Mario indicated the full beanery with a small pessimistic shrug. Matt pressed a one pound note into the waiter's hand and suddenly a table became available right opposite the happy couple.

'Ignore him,' Lily muttered to Tom as Matt was sat down. 'He's not well.'

'Who's not well?' the Invalid demanded loudly, causing some adjacent diners to sit up and take notice.

'He certainly doesn't ler-look very well,' Tom agreed.

The Invalid leant over the intervening table and waved a bread stick at Lily.

'Listen,' he said. 'Tell your Doctor friend – when I want his swot ideas I'll pay for them.'

'He's National Health,' said Lily.

The Invalid sat back and wiping his fevered brow with a napkin rose, bared his teeth in the semblance of a smile.

'So go on then. Don't mind me,' he continued, essaying a quick change of tactics. 'Enjoy yourselves. Relish your little tête à tête, your billet doux, your moment of magic. I'm not here. Pretend I don't exist.'

'I think I'll have the chicken breasts in butter and garlic,' said Lily to Tom, trying to ignore her demented partner.

'Don't expect to work with me if you're going to eat garlic,' Matt informed her.

'He really should be in bed,' said Lily.

'How can I possibly be in bed when she's wearing my sheets?' Matt roared in appeal to the by now riveted adjacent diners.

Tom half leant anxiously towards Matt.

'Mr Ber-Browne. Has Ler-Lily done anything to upset you?'

'Upset me?' croaked Matt. 'Lionel? Lionel couldn't upset me. Just because she doesn't arrive for work, and when she does it's in provocative clothes to go out to lunch with her inamorata, then she comes back and takes the clothes off my bed and goes out to lunch again with her inamorata –'

Tom frowned.

'Inam – inam – inam –'

Lily put a hand on Tom's arm to stop him.

'Why should my having lunch with Tom upset you?' she asked Matt.

'Upset me?' said Matt, breaking his bread stick into one million pieces. 'What makes you think it upsets me?'

'I can't imagine,' Lily replied.

Matt proceeded to annihilate another bread stick.

'Because,' he said.

'Because?'

Matt, unable to look at her, raised his voice instead.

'*Because*. I – like you.'

Lily smiled.

'I like you, too.'

'Don't be ridiculous!' Matt roared. 'How can you like *me* and go out and have a cosy little lunch with *him*? Obviously you really like him.'

'Of course I *really* like him. I've really liked him for as long as I can remember.'

'Oh you have, have you?' hooted Matt, rising to his feet.

The whole restaurant was now transfixed.

'Well,' he continued, swaying slightly as the fever gripped him further. 'Well I happen to – *really* like you as well, Lionel.'

Lily smiled at him.

'And I like you very much.'

'I quite ler-like you too,' added Tom for good measure.

'You just keep out of this, Doctor Strabismus!'

Matt leant further across the table towards Lily.

'This is ridiculous. If you like me, and since I like you, you can't go round liking him as *well*.'

He jerked a thumb in Tom's direction.

'Why ever not?' asked Lily. 'He's my brother.'

CHAPTER THREE

I've grown accustomed to your salad cream sandwiches.

One week later, when Lily had recovered her dress and Matt had recovered from his ague, a rendezvous was made between them in order to start work on Lily's play. They were both, separately, full of hope, Matt as he sat eating his perfectly prepared bachelor breakfast and doing *The Times* crossword and Lily as she bicycled happily across Clapham Common. The Spring weather was perfect, Matt's egg was correctly cooked and Lily's back tyre was utterly airtight. The initial skirmishes had been fought and honourably drawn, and the field was now clear for them to concentrate on the main campaign – that of getting the play into shape and shaping the play into a musical. What could possibly go wrong now? Lily thought as she tucked her Bugs Bunny tee shirt into her faded blue jeans preparatory to pressing Matt's doorbell. Here she was, fully equipped to start work, sano in mens and sano in corpora *and* twenty-five minutes early. Everything was definitely set fair.

'You're early,' said Matt as he opened the door, suddenly distempered by her premature arrival.

'Oh,' said a startled Lily, left standing in the doorway as Matt returned to his unfinished breakfast.

'Not only early, but very early.'

Lily crossed the room and was just about to deposit her bulging carrier on top of the grand piano when a look from above the top of *The Times* warned her of her impending folly.

'If grand pianos were meant to hold carrier bags,' said Matt, 'there would be places to hang them.'

Lily spotted a furled knob on the side of the instrument and neatly hooked her luggage on to it.

'Comme si?' she enquired, starting to unpack.

Matt rattled his paper irritably, annoyed by the score.

Lily looked round at him, and caught him reaching for his fried egg bap.

'Are you having breakfast?'

'No I'm tunnelling through the Alps.'

Lily felt sure that the clouds would soon lift from Mr Music and that once more all would be brightness and light. After all it was such a lovely day. Perhaps he was just a bad starter.

She smiled at him and, unpacking some assorted plastic food boxes from her carrier, sat down opposite. He took no notice and continued to eat his bap fastidiously while doing *The Times* crossword with alarming alacrity. Lily pulled a little face at the man concealed behind the news, then from her boxes produced a jar of mayonnaise, a plastic beaker with plastic top and some slices of bread in a clear plastic wrapper. She spread them out on the table between them.

Matt, having finished his first egg bap, put down his paper and reached for his second.

'Pass me those scissors, would you?' he requested Lily, since they were just out of his reach.

Lily pushed them across to him, then watched in astonishment as he proceeded ultra carefully to trim off the white of the egg which was overlapping the side of the bap. Matt looked up and caught her staring at him. She quickly averted her gaze and turned her attention to the preparation of her own breakfast.

It was now Matt's turn to be astonished, if that is a sufficient enough description of the feeling he entertained as he watched Lily pouring vast amounts of salad cream between thickly buttered steps of bread before concluding the confection by a selection of pickled gherkins. And it was Lily's turn to catch Matt staring in bewilderment at her. She gave him a small smile, but he simply continued to gape goggle eyed. Then, pushing his egg-bap away from him in disgust, he stood up and walked across to the window where he remained for some time, silently contemplating the world below.

'Is this your normal breakfast?' he finally enquired of her.

'Not really,' replied Lily.

Matt's shoulders relaxed in visible relief.

'I forgot the banana.'

The shoulders restiffened. Lily shrugged to herself and poured out some coffee.

'And the beetroot,' she added. 'They're all full of goodness.'

The back remained firmly turned towards her, still emanating hostility.

'And another thing,' he said, 'Exactly what have you got on?'

Lily had to admit to herself that this question found her wanting. She appraised her appearance – jeans, Bugs Bunny and horrid cardy – and wondered why on earth El Capo should require some comment from her about her dress.

'Just some comfortable working clothes,' she offered.

'They are hardly what *I* would call comfortable working clothes,' replied the back, crisply. 'Kindly wear something a little more appropriate next time.'

Lily stuck her hand out in Nazi salute and clicked her silent heels.

'Yah wohl, mein Fuhrer.'

But Matt turned and caught her in full pose. If looks could kill, thought Lily, she had just died young.

The Maestro began to pace up and down, so Lily, fearful that this indicated an immediate intention to work, bolted the rest of her salad cream sandwich and packed up her debris.

The pacing up and down continued for two or three silent minutes, then The Thinker stopped right in front of her and for the first time that day looked The Listener right in the eyes.

'Love,' he said.

Lily's heart ridiculously skipped a beat.

'I want to talk to you this morning about falling in love.'

This was followed by another long silence. On top of a skipping heart, Lily now felt the beginnings of an acute bout of acid indigestion, brought on no doubt by her over anxious consumption of the last mayonnaise and gherkin confection.

Matt walked away from her and stared once more out of the window.

'Yes, falling in love,' he mused.

No, it wasn't indigestion. It was a much more inexplicable

sensation which Lily was experiencing, as if she had just swallowed a handful of butterflies. Why should he want to talk about love? And with her? Blindly she poured herself out another cup of coffee.

'You are pouring coffee into the sugar bowl,' Matt observed.

'So I am,' agreed Lily. 'I've got very sweet teeth.'

'Perhaps we can get back to falling in love?'

'Of course we can,' hastened Lily, stirring her syrupy beverage. 'But of course.'

Matt began to pace again.

'Right. Well – it just isn't on.'

Lily spilt a dash of coffee right down Bugs Bunny.

'Who said it was?'

'Will you just keep quiet and *listen*? This ridiculous love business – as you see it. Opening a door, seeing each other for the very first time and the whole world standing still. It just isn't on.'

'Oh.'

The butterflies turned to salt fossils. Lily busied herself with the final packing up of her breakfast things, in order to appear as nonchalant as possible.

'Don't you believe in coup de foudre, Mr Browne?'

'I most certainly do not.'

'Why not?'

'Because I haven't the foggiest idea what it means.'

Lily looked up at him, expecting to see him smile. Instead he was frowning earnestly down at her.

'The clap of thunder,' she explained. 'Love at first sight.'

Matt turned on his heel.

'Phooey.'

'Speak for yourself,' defended Lily.

'But I am not speaking for myself,' concluded Matt. '*I* – am speaking about your play.'

Silence. What a soft goal!

'My *play*? You're speaking about my play?'

'What did you think I was speaking about?'

'I thought – you were speaking about my play.'

Lily drank deeply from the sugar bowl. Either the man was a brilliant gamesman or an out and out sadist.

'So. You don't like my play?'

'Your play is fine. Except for the way the two principal

characters meet and fall in love and what they say to each other and what they do and how they do it, your play is fine.'

'That *is* my play.'

'Well – the rest of it's fine.'

He was a sadist.

The telephone rang, interrupting the silence.

'That's your telephone.'

'I can recognise my telephone,' he said, picking up a large sea shell and holding it to his ear.

'You probably notice I have quite a sense of humour as well,' he added, replacing the ornament and picking up the telephone. 'Though it's not always this visible.'

'I can believe that,' Lily muttered.

Matt listened to the voice on the phone and then slowly turned to Lily. He handed her the receiver.

'It's your mother.'

'My *mother*?'

'And it's too early to start drinking.'

Matt shook his head as Lily hissed into the telephone.

'Ma? I can't talk now, Ma. I'm meant to be at work – what? Yes, I'm fine. Fine, but I must get back to work. What? Oh all right.'

She held the phone away from her and leant towards Matt.

'Granny wants a quick word.'

Matt took the receiver.

'Not with you,' said Lily taking it back. 'With me. Hello Littlema?'

Matt sank to the sofa and put his head in his hands. He stared at his Hush Puppies and hated them more deeply than ever.

'Yes I'm fine,' Lily burbled, 'Fine. No – he hasn't tried to take advantage of me, Littlema. Not yet, anyway.'

She flashed her breeziest of smiles at Matt who remained immoveably appalled.

'Yes of course, Littlema. I'll be careful. 'Bye.'

Lily returned the receiver to its cradle and wished the floor would open up.

'That was my Little Grannie,' she offered lamely.

'I don't care if it was The Green Giant! Now may we get *on*?'

'Of course.'

Lily sat down obediently and ferreted in her carrier for her new Venus H.B.s.

'Shoot.'

Matt at once resumed his pacing.

'Right,' he said. 'We are here to work. Right?'

Lily nodded in keen agreement.

'Right,' she answered.

'Right,' continued Matt, breathing in deeply. 'Right.'

'Right,' said Lily.

'Will you stop saying right?'

Lily pulled a small face.

'Right.'

Matt looked stonily at her.

'Right.'

'We sound like an army marching on one foot,' said Lily brightly. 'Right, right – right, right. Like that riddle. What goes ninety-nine bonk? A centipede with a wooden – '

Matt interrupted warningly.

'Lily!'

'A centipede with a wooden Lily?'

Lily decided as she caught an even stonier look that she might as well give up. Nothing was getting through, perhaps because El Capo liked to keep his mind purely on the matters in hand.

'Can we please get on?' he asked her. 'Concentrate. Right? Just concentrate.'

Lily frowned in attempted concentration.

'Right.'

'Right.'

'Bonk.'

She could have bitten her uncontrollable tongue off as Matt rose in explosive fury.

'I cannot possibly work if you keep distracting me! Will you just please try and concentrate? Why is it that women just cannot concentrate?'

'Probably because we've always got something better to do,' Lily replied, immediately regretting it. Could she say nothing right this morning?

Matt began once more to pace feverishly about.

'Just try it for once,' he pleaded. 'Try concentrating. Just for once.'

Lily was well known for her willingness to try anything once. In fact her form mistress had once marked her school report with the words: 'Lily is a trier – and she would succeed more if she tried less hard'. However, today, for her newly found partner, she would give it all she'd got. And so, for what seemed like an eternity, they both sat silent, staring intently into the middle distance.

After one million light years, Lily felt in need of nourishment, so she quietly sneaked two bananas out of her carrier and proffered one to the Maestro. He regarded it with ill concealed disgust.

'I do not like bananas,' he said.

'Don't have it then.'

'I won't. I don't like people *eating* bananas either.'

'Ah,' replied Lily. 'Then don't look.'

'I can *feel* when somebody is eating a banana.'

There was no answer to this, Lily realised as she contemplated her half peeled fruit. So she rummaged in her carrier and produced a roll of scotch tape.

'So,' said Matt. 'Where were we?'

'Could I borrow your scissors please?'

Matt passed her the scissors, but instead of being able to continue with his train of thought he found himself totally sidetracked by Lily's attempts to reseal her banana with the Sellotape.

'What are you *doing*?'

Lily smiled up at him.

'Zipping up my banana. Black is beautiful, but not on a banana. I'll have it later.'

And with that she replaced it in her bag.

'Right.'

She was all ready to go again.

'No more distractions?' Matt asked warily.

'I am all yours, mon capitaine,' smiled Lily cheerfully.

He regarded her suspiciously.

'I can't work with all these distractions, you know.'

'I know.'

The doorbell rang.

'That's your doorbell.'

'I know it's my doorbell!' said Matt, picking up his phone. 'I don't need you to tell me what my doorbell sounds like.'

'Then why are you answering the phone?'

Matt replaced the telephone furiously. What was this girl doing to him?

He glared at her and went to answer the door. Lily stretched and yawned deeply. She felt quite worn out with all this concentrating. She wiggled her toes inside her sneakers and realised that there was a lot more to this writing business than met the eye.

Matt returned, holding out in front of him extremely distastefully a mynah bird in a cage.

'Yours, I believe,' he said icily.

Lily looked from the bird to Matt then back again to the bird.

'Yes,' she agreed. 'That's Jacky Boy.'

She peered more closely at her pet.

'Are you better then?' she asked him. 'He must be better then.'

Matt hopped from one foot to the other.

'I don't care if he's about to pop his stupid cork! I am not working with this around the place. What the hell's it doing here anyway?'

'I suppose Tom must have dropped it round.'

'A man in a uniform dropped it round. A hospital porter or something. What is it doing here?'

'Well. You see. He's been ill. He's had this frightful cough and a friend of my brother Tom – you remember Tom – well he's a vet – not Tom, his chum, and he's been mending Jacky. They said they weren't going to drop him round till later.'

Silence. Matt looked with unbridled animosity at the black bird which promptly responded with a nasty cough. Blondes, bananas, birds. All B's. He couldn't cope any more. B's were usually pleasant easy going things, like butterflies, books and beds. Not banana eating blondes with black birds. He took an extra deep breath in an attempt to regain his poise.

'Cover him up and let's get on with it, for God's sake.'

'You can't cover him up. If you cover him up he only does his classified results.'

'Don't be absurd,' Matt retorted, throwing a large tea towel over the cage. 'Now. Where were we?'

'Liverpool two, Arsenal one,' said a voice from under the tea towel. 'Liverpool two – '

Matt picked up the cage determinedly. Lily looked at him with apprehension.

'You're not going to do anything Jacky might regret?' she asked.

'No,' said Matt. 'I am going to shut him in the kitchen. Right?'

'Wrong,' Lily muttered as Matt disappeared into the kitchen and her fear was realised as Jacky emitted a piercing scream from the depths of the galley.

It wasn't long before Matt reappeared still carrying the rebellious bird. Lily smiled sheepishly at him, although she had never once in her life seen a sheep smile.

'Sorry,' she murmured. 'But he doesn't like being on his Jack Jones.'

'Then kindly shut him up,' directed Matt.

'Shut up, Jacky.'

'Shut up, Jacky,' parroted the mynah, if such things are possible.

Lily turned her back on the cage.

'Best thing to do is to ignore him,' she said. 'Now where were we?'

'We were talking,' Matt replied through tightly closed teeth, 'about the way two people fall in *love*.'

The convalescent bird coughed loudly.

'Poor old Jacky boy,' said Lily solicitously, before she caught El Capo's angry eye. 'Sorry.'

'In this play you have written, we are agreed, are we not – ?'

'I shouldn't think so for one moment.'

'We are *agreed* that the way the man and woman fall in love is utterly ridiculous.'

Lily didn't remember agreeing to any such thing.

'Why?' she ventured.

'Don't ask so many damn questions!' Matt shouted. 'You know perfectly well! It's like saying . . . It's like saying . . . '

He foundered as he noticed Lily's large eyes staring into him. He also noticed that such a stare gave him a most extraordinary feeling.

'Look,' he continued. 'It's as if someone like – '

Here he gestured vaguely in her direction.

'If you want to take it to its most preposterous extremes . . . should – '

Another vague gesture.

'With someone like me. And that as soon as we met, we just went – '

'Clang clang, Hong Kong,' chimed Jacky.

Lily thought for a moment that her bird's future was in serious jeopardy, but Matt managed to control his volcanic feelings.

'Why is that so preposterous?' Lily asked, anxious to keep the ball rolling.

'Why is what so preposterous?'

'What you just said.'

'Because. Because things like that just do not happen. That is why!'

'Yes they do,' contradicted Lily. 'Look at History. History is full of such cases.'

'Special cases.'

'Romeo and Juliet, Antony and Cleopatra . . . Hank and Maggie.'

Matt looked at her, astounded.

'*Who* – are Hank and Maggie?'

'Two friends of mine,' Lily replied. 'They met and fell in love bowling for a pig.'

With which her protagonist sank slowly to the sofa and put his head in his hands. From the ensuing silence and the Antarctic atmosphere, Lily realised she had strayed too far.

'Go home,' said her mentor. 'Go home and take your carrots, your sarnies, your mayonnaise, your pickled gherkins, your family phone calls, your riddles, your jokes, your parrot – '

'My mynah bird.'

'Will you stop correcting my grammar? Just go home – and don't you come back until you're prepared to take things seriously! There is no way that I can work with you like this! Right?'

'Right.'

Lily collected her belongings, picked up her bird cage and made her way to the front door. She gave one look round to him in the forlorn hope that he was teasing, or in case he might have relented, but no, still he sat, head nursed in hands, emanating fury. She closed the door behind her. It had started out as such a lovely day.

Over the subsequent rain-swept summer days, Matt's anguish and self loathing abated not one bit. On the contrary, never before had he felt so much disgust at his inability to play life's cards in any sort of acceptable order. Always and forever, when it came to the crunch, he blew it. There seemed to be some mechanism built in to him, constantly programmed to self destruct, so that whenever he was faced with the possibility of a promising relationship, instead of behaving in the accepted heterosexual manner, he annihilated the potential co-habitant with a laser beam of aggressive vituperation. And now he had done it in spades. He had just sent packing one of the most innocent and heart warming of female creatures he had ever had the good fortune to meet. He did not even deserve to entertain the thought that one day she might forget, forgive and return to pick up the pieces.

So one particularly wet morning when he sat having a more than usually disconsolate breakfast, dejectedly filling in *The Times* crossword, and when his doorbell rang at two minutes to nine he did not even bother to consider who the caller might be, so non-existent were his expectations. With the consequence that when he discovered a cycling-caped Lily waiting in the corridor he was so ill prepared that he found himself once more retreating into aggression.

'If you are suddenly going to turn up after all, there is no need to get here *right* on time,' he snapped as he heard his grandfather clock strike nine.

But on this particular morning, Lily Pond was well prepared for anything the enemy might try throwing at her out of the trenches and with the briefest – indeed she hoped curtest – of nods, she brushed past him into the sitting room.

Matt closed the door and remembered his nightly repeated vow to try and behave in a more humane fashion.

'Lovely day,' he jibed, in an effort to lighten the atmosphere.

Lily took off her sou'wester and remembered her own undertaking to ignore her mentor's snideries. So she merely removed her cape, adjusted her efficiently tucked up hair, and with a businesslike smile crossed determinedly to the sofa.

'What I meant,' muttered Matt, still trying to recover lost ground, 'What I meant was there was no need for you to get here *right* on time.'

How did he know that she was coming back at all? Lily asked herself and she sat down and unclipped her dead father's old school brief case. Perhaps he was one of those geniuses blessed with second sight.

How did he know that she was coming back at all? Matt asked himself, regretting his thoughtless form of conversation. What must she think of his presumption. He clicked his tongue and crossed to look out of the window into the street below. She can't have thought he was that bad, he postulated, because at least she had come back.

He turned round to find her setting out rows of Biros, notebooks, erasers, hole punchers and staplers on his coffee table. He stared vacantly at the display, at a loss for words.

'Ready,' she said.

'Ready? Ready for what?'

'Ready.'

She looked at him, secretary-like, unsmiling. And it was then he first noticed her outfit. Demure sensible grey knitted two piece with a Gor-ray skirt, lisle stockings and heavy duty brogues.

'What are you dressed like that for?' he asked. 'You look like something on the front of a knitting pattern.'

Lily remembered her vow and ignored him.

'Whenever you're ready,' she replied.

'Ready? Ready for what? You keep asking me whenever I'm ready.'

Lily looked up at him.

'Ready – for work.'

She then supplied him with the briefest of smiles, a smile well practised in front of her mirror over the last few days and guaranteed to chill the heart.

'I've made some notes about what we were talking about the other day – ' she continued, while looking for them. 'Here we are. Yes. About love.'

So far so good, Lily thought. Everything was going according to the carefully rehearsed plan. Even down to the perplexity she happily noted on Matt's face as it was his turn to be wrong footed.

'Love?' he crunked. 'And what do you know about love?'

She had anticipated he would become aggressive at this point, so she decided to relax him with a warm smile. As soon as she saw him relaxed, she shut the door in his face by switching off the warmth.

'I was thinking that obviously you would have had much more experience in the field than I have – '

'No I haven't!'

Lily searched for her mother's spectacles and putting them on pretended to study her partner carefully. She was glad to observe that he was sweating slightly on that high domed forehead of his.

'Sorry,' she said. 'You were saying?'

'I was saying – what makes you think I have had all this experience?'

'Men are *always* more experienced than women in those fields.'

'So who do men get all their experience *with*?'

'Yes,' she conceded, 'Yes, I hadn't thought of that.'

'You will do when you're a mother.'

Two all. That'll teach her to play four two four. She decided to bring on a substitute.

'Anyway. That's what I thought we should concentrate on today.'

'You did?'

'I did.'

The substitute had warmed up and was now allowed on the field. Lily took off her glasses and leant forward, putting her chin on one carefully cupped hand.

Matt recognised a change of tactics, but was unable to identify the ploy.

'So?' he had to ask. 'So what are you doing now?'

'Concentrating.'

A roar came up from the terraces as the ball hit the back of the net.

Matt regarded his opponent in silence. Then sat down. Silence crowned silence. It became almost deafening.

'It's no good!'

He suddenly jumped to his feet.

'I can't concentrate like this! Why can't you just relax?'

'I am relaxed. Look – I'm perfectly relaxed.'

'No you are not! Otherwise you wouldn't be sitting there – all like that!'

Matt hopped up and down now like a scalded bean . . . Lily tried to look at him evenly but it was becoming harder by the moment.

'How am I sitting?'

The realisation that he was being outplayed gave Matt an overlarge rush of blood to the head.

'How do *I* know how you're sitting?' he expostulated.

'Only you can tell how you're sitting. But I'll tell you one thing. You are not sitting as if you were *relaxed*. Relaxed people sit – all – relaxed. Not like you. What's the matter with you? I don't know what's got into you. You arrive here looking as if Caesar's conquered Gaul and there's no butter in the shops, dressed like the great aunt of an ailing archbishop with an attitude of mind that would hardly befit a depression on a weather chart! And I'm expected to work alongside of this? Relax. Stop taking it all so *seriously*.'

Lily looked up at him sharply.

'Say a riddle,' he continued. 'Have a mayonnaise sandwich. Ring your parrot.'

'Mynah bird.'

'Whatever – but for God's sake do *something*.'

'I am doing something,' said Lily patiently. 'I am trying to work.'

'All right! All *right*! We'll work. If that's what you want to do, we'll work.'

He started to pace about the room in his now traditional fashion. Lily picked up a finely sharpened H.B. and her notebook in anticipation.

But Matt stopped by the end of the sofa and pointed his Biro at her.

'Your idea of love, and my idea of love are about as far apart as Istanbul and Constantinople.'

'They're one and the same place,' Lily informed him.

'Good,' said Matt, 'I was just testing you. They are about as far apart as Leningrad and St Petersburg – '

'*They're one* – '

He jabbed his Biro into her shoulder.

'May I finish? Our views on love are about as far apart as Leningrad and St Petersburg, Massachusetts.'

He removed the Biro and gave her a concessionary nod. She looked suitably abashed. The penalty was deserved.

Matt resumed his pacing, glowing with success.

'You see,' he informed her. 'You believe love happens like a clap of thunder, while I believe the opposite. I believe love happens like – '

'Like a pat of powder puffs?'

He didn't even bother to stop and glare at her, so pathetic was her attempt at a tackle.

'That it happens in its own good time,' he continued.

'Furthermore, I do not believe that people go around saying to each other the things *you* have them saying at the beginning of this!'

He waved her manuscript dramatically.

'In real life people say . . . people say – isn't it cold out and can I get you a taxi? They do not say – '

He sat down at the end of the sofa and looked at her.

'They do not say "you-and-I-were-meant-for-each-other, I-have-never-seen-a-vision-quite-so-lovely, I-don't-know-what-I-did-before-I-met-you, I-love-you and you-have-the-starlight-in-your-eyes".'

He stopped as suddenly as he had begun. Their eyes met and there was silence.

Lily cleared her throat.

'They don't say that in my play.'

'Things like that.'

'They don't.'

'Don't they?'

'No.'

'Things like that,' muttered Matt.

Lily shifted her position slightly.

'She says to him – ' she tried again. 'She says to him that he is the most ridiculous and impossible person she has ever met, yet he lights up the night when she is with him and that before she met him every day was like a Monday morning.'

Matt still stared at her, then he broke away and leafed through the manuscript.

'I don't remember that bit.'

'I jotted it in last night,' Lily said quickly, knowing that it was nowhere to be found on the typed pages.

'And what does he say?' he asked suspiciously.

'Nothing,' said Lily. 'He can't.'

Again she thought she must have gone too far, kicked him too hard on the shins or pushed him too brutally in the back, because his face had suffused with colour and his large eyes had opened even wider than ever.

'Ridiculous!' he snorted. 'Absurd. Why can't he? He can't just stand there saying nothing. Of course he can say something.'

Lily shook her head, unshakeable in her belief.

'He can't.'

'Of course he can! He'd say . . . he'd say . . . '

Matt inhaled deeply, but the breath would not come, and so anguished was he with paralysing shyness that he became totally word-bound. He picked a cushion up from the sofa and began beating it rhythmically against the arm of a chair. Then when that therapy failed to free him from his word block, he picked up the manuscript of her play and hurled it against the wall. Lily looked anxiously at him, then quietly began to pack up her things.

'I think I'd better go home,' she said.

Which instantly freed Matt from his silence.

'What are you talking about?'

'I said,' Lily repeated gently, 'I think I'd better go home.'

She stood up and looked at him.

'You're right.'

'What am I right about now?' he demanded.

Lily gave him a brave but small smile and continued her packing. She realised that any further truck with this particular man in this particular mood was about as pointless as trying to sail the ocean in a colander.

'I just think I'd better go home, that's all.'

She looked up and found him staring wildly at her. Then he suddenly made a dash for the front door and locked it, removing the key.

'What are you doing?' Lily asked, in a certain amount of trepidation. She had an intense dislike of being locked into places.

'We'll see!' was Matt's half choked answer. 'We'll soon see who can and who can't! We'll see!'

And pointing a spiky finger in her direction he rushed into his bedroom and locked the door behind him.

Lily stared in bewilderment and anxiety at the barricade, then went and cautiously tried the handle. It was locked. She tried the front door. That was very locked as well. So she sat herself down on the sofa and took ten deep breaths to stop herself panicking. Being locked in places by strange people who behaved irrationally and pointed demented fingers at one was enough to induce a sense of alarm in those most phlegmatic of souls, among whose number Lily most certainly did not count herself. Perhaps it was only a temporary aberration on the part of her mentor. Lily picked up a copy of her play and began half-heartedly to flick through it. Yes, perhaps it was just a temporary rush of blood to the head and in a minute he would walk out wreathed in smiles. And then when she recollected the pattern of his behaviour ever since they had first met, she realised there was faint hope of such a resolution to this present chapter of events. More likely he was going to starve her into submission. So she curled herself up on the sofa and, sighing a heart felt sigh, longed for the safety of her little room at home.

Matt replaced the telephone and tip-toed across the bedroom to have another check on his prisoner through the keyhole. Apparently from what he could see she was fast asleep, which confirmed one of his many opinions about the opposite sex. Namely that in times of crises women put their heads under their wings and slept right through them. Still, she'd find it difficult to doze right through this one, that is provided everything went according to plan. He rubbed his hands in anticipation, then sat on his bed and curled his legs up under him. Yes, provided he had the patience and everything worked out as it should do. Miss Lily Pond should know exactly what was what by the end of the day.

Exactly one hour and three quarters later the doorbell rang. At once Matt, who had barely moved during those long minutes of waiting, was on his feet and across to the keyhole. She was still asleep. The doorbell rang again and he saw his sleeping beauty stir in her slumber and sit up, rubbing her eyes and looking about her, trying to get her bearings. The bell rang yet again.

'Matt?' she called. 'Matt? There's someone at your door!'

Matt stood up from the keyhole and leant his back against the door. He could hardly breathe for the excitement.

'Matt!' his prisoner called once more. 'The door!'

'You go!' he suddenly answered.

The sound of his voice temporarily disconcerted Lily and she looked about her, still confused.

'What?'

'You go!' he shouted. 'You go to the door!'

'Why can't you?'

'Because I can't!'

Lily shrugged and trundled over to the door. Stranger and stranger, she thought, Alice-like. Did he have a thing about answering his own front door as well?

She turned the handle on the door, forgetting it was locked. 'It's locked!' she called.

Matt cursed under his breath. He hadn't accounted for that. Then he heard her shouting at the unknown caller, saving him from having to show his face. The last thing he wanted to do was show his face, as he was hopeless at concealing anything and he knew he would at once give the game away.

'I can't open it!' Lily was shouting. 'It's locked whoever you are!'

Lily was down on her knees, trying to communicate through the letter box.

'Telegram,' replied a voice.

'Oh,' said Lily. 'Then bung it through here then.'

A small brown envelope was shoved through, which Lily was forced to receive in her mouth.

'Charming,' she said.

'You're welcome,' replied the departing voice.

Lily stood up and was about to read the envelope when she suddenly realised it would be a purely academic exercise since only one person lived here. So she crossed to the bedroom and called through the locked door.

'Matt? Telegram.'

'Is it for me?'

Lily sighed.

'Well of course it's for you! Who do you think it's for, me? It's hardly likely to be for me!'

She looked at the envelope and received her first carefully Matt-calculated surprise. The telegram was for her.

'It's for me!'

'So open it then!' ordered her janitor.

Lily scratched the top of her head.

'Who on earth would send me a telegram here?'

'Open it!' Matt rasped, getting cross. 'Open it and find out!'

It was exactly the same when you gave them presents, Matt thought as he took another peek through the keyhole. They always stood holding the gift wrapped parcel while wondering out loud what was inside.

'It can't be the pools because I forgot to post my coupon,' she was muttering to herself. 'And anyway I don't live here.'

'OPEN IT!'

Lily opened it and read it. Matt tried to catch a glimpse of her face through his spyhole but she had turned away from him. Instead all he got was silence.

Then she spoke.

'It's from you.'

Matt leaned his forehead against the bedroom door, suddenly exhausted.

'So-what-does-it-say?' he asked her through the crack.

'I love you,' said Lily.

Matt leant against the door, and then unlocked it.

He came out and without looking at her walked slowly past her to the centre of the room. Then he took a deep sigh and rubbed his hands on the sides of his trousers.

'*Now* can we get on?' he asked her.

Lily came to his side, smiling that particular smile which had probably initiated the whole fantastic chain of events.

'You might at least have made it greetings,' she said.

CHAPTER FOUR

Cupboard Love

The fact that Matt had sent her a telegram communicating his most tenderest of feelings to her should have given Lily an all permeating sense of satisfaction, not to mention elation. No one knew this better than Lily herself. She not only knew this. She was only too well aware of it and it was this very awareness that made her even more utterly miserable. At the precise moment of a girl's life when she should be leap frogging over parking meters, and swinging from low hanging branches, as per all the romantic films she had ever caught a flickering glimpse of on the family's 1947 Bush television, all she actually felt like doing was falling on her metaphorical sword. Hardly appropriate in the circumstances.

She opened the front door with her latch key, as quietly as she could, hoping by some miracle that she would find herself alone in the house, her grandmother and her mother inexplicably whisked away, and solitude, sweet solitude, alone there to greet her in the warm, worn rooms that made up their family spread. No such luck. She could already hear her mother's voice raised in mild protestation at some remark that Littlema had made, and her grandmother's answering retort.

'Pooh. Second at seven to one. Not enough to keep us in tea leaves. When will somebody tell these imbecile horses there is no point in coming second?'

Oh môche – Littlema had lost again on the horses. That meant another of those jolly little suppers together when she took out her teeth and then fell asleep before the News at Ten, leaving Lily to try and take off her glasses without waking her up. Still, at least it wasn't the other way round. Small mercies. Lily sighed before pushing the kitchen door open and plunging into the fray. She knew it wasn't like her not to feel like 'la vie familiale' and she supposed she should blame it on the fact that she had had such a hard week with Matt. Day after day locked in the same old room, with the same old flocked wallpaper and the same old Harrods furniture could get anyone down, however devoted they were to their work or, in this particular case – to her play, but somehow it had all changed in the last few weeks, since the telegram.

'I give up betting horses and now I bet on certainty. That your Lily will be in for supper on a Friday night. What is my granddaughter? When I was her age we had the entire Russian cavalry at our house.'

'Of course you did, Mother. They were hiding from the Poles.'

Lily could hear the familiar early evening clatter as her mother flew round the kitchen, and the equally familiar tension in her mother's voice as she tried not get impatient with Littlema.

She pushed the door open.

'Hiding from the Poles, *stuff*. Our cavalry never hid from the Poles.'

'Everybody in their right minds hides from the Poles,' replied her mother, who had an in-built prejudice against them since they had once had a Polish lodger during the war who used to pinch their rations.

'Anything of interest for supper?'

Littlema patted her nose with a fine lace handkerchief, and then sniffed, which was a habit she had when she was about to say something disapproving, but on this particular occasion gave Lily the opportunity to pinch her evening paper.

'Ah.'

Littlema sniffed again, in case Lily had not heard the first one.

'So you're in for supper again?'

'If it's anything like last night's rabbit pie, in-for's the operative word.'

'It wasn't rabbit pie, Lily,' said Mrs Pond, trying not to look offended. 'It was chicken casserole.'

'You weren't here to eat it.'

Lily rolled her eyes and then squinted at her mother to make her laugh.

'And you should not be here to eat it tonight,' retorted Littlema quickly. 'When I was your age child – '

'Not another dancing with four archdukes at the Winter Palace speech?'

'You people,' Littlema sniffed for the third time. 'What is wrong with you people?'

'I put it down to this terrible shortage of granddukes in Streatham, Littlema,' said Lily.

'Why don't you go and turn on the television, Mother?'

'Yes, why don't you, Littlema?'

Her grandmother pulled her shawl tighter round her shoulders and, having clearly run out of sniffs, snorted instead.

'I refuse to be treated like a child. Just because I am old and losing my mind.'

'It's Argentina versus West Germany this evening, Littlema. You don't want to miss that, do you?' Lily coaxed.

Victory was close at hand, until Littlema's eyes fell on her evening paper, which her daughter had filled with potato peelings.

'So what you do to my evening paper?' wailed the old lady. 'Before I even see my horoscope.'

'Mother ' said Mrs Pond, flapping a teatowel at the air. 'If there is anything surprising left in store for you, then why not let it surprise you? Now go and watch your cricket.'

'Cricket, stuff.'

Littlema shuffled out.

'If someone would just tell me what is wrong with you people.'

'It's too much white bread, that's what the trouble is,' murmured Lily, vainly attempting to read her own horoscope in the now soggy paper. 'So – let's see what's in store for me . . . if anything. Pisces. "A routine day, but a surprise in the evening." Oh yes. "Romance and fresh adventure with your loved one." All I can say Katina dear is you don't know Mr Matthew Browne.'

Lily looked at her mother dolefully. Her mother looked back at her equally dolefully from the looking glass behind the kitchen door where she appeared to be busy trying to stick a hatpin into the side of her ear.

'So still he doesn't ask you out?'

Lily tried to smile and failed.

'So still he doesn't ask me out,' she agreed.

'A beautiful girl like you. There must be something wrong in his wires. Now.'

The hatpin having emerged at a rakish angle at the other side of her hat, Mrs Pond took off her apron.

'Now.'

'What have I got? Two heads or something?'

Lily looked at her mother pleadingly. In a way if she answered her in the affirmative, it would at least give her a solid reason for Matt's behaviour. After all some men probably didn't like women with two heads, just as some men didn't like redheads. The question of whether or not her daughter had two heads was, however, obviously too heavy a question for Mrs Pond to tackle at this particular point of the evening, because she just frowned vaguely and told Lily not to talk in riddles and not to let her grandmother have too much salt. After which injunctions she disappeared like the White Rabbit muttering about the time and whether or not she had enough change for the bus.

Lily watched her go with mixed feelings. It was always the same with mothers. When you really needed them they always had a bus to catch, or their sewing machine had broken down. And when you didn't need them they fussed round you like an old mother hen, wrapping you in Pure New Wool on the hottest days and insisting on your having a Hot Meal just before you ran for your train.

Môche.

Her mother stuck her head round the kitchen door again.

'I forgot to tell you Lily, the mince is in the oven.'

She started to go out again.

'Ma?'

Lily wasn't letting her off the hook so easily.

'Do you think it's because we're always in his flat? I mean do you think maybe because we're always just in his flat, he only looks on me as his writing partner? Do you think if I can get him out of there, maybe things might be different?'

'Maybe,' agreed Mrs Pond, with what seemed to Lily an extraordinary lack of interest in her daughter's affairs of the heart. 'Now I must fly. You know what the buses are like.'

'Big, and red, and very infrequent.'

It was too familiar a joke for both of them for either to smile and Mrs Pond departed at last. Lily paused on her way over to the oven to think how much they all took her mother for granted. The way she cooked and cleaned all afternoon, before departing without a grumble for her evening job. God bless mums, even if they weren't much good at doling out advice for the lovelorn. 'Incroyable,' she thought as she removed the cover from the casserole. And this was *mince*? She put the lid back hastily and shut the oven door. It was preferable to return to her P for problems, or rather M for Matt-type problems. Was she on to the right line? Did Matt just need taking out of himself? Would a sudden change in the routine of their relationship make all the difference? Please, please, please help it to be that. Do not write on both sides of the paper at once, do not pass go, do not collect two hundred.

'Go out? What do you want to go out for? There's nothing to be gained by going out.'

Matt was reacting to Lily's suggestion like a Cistercian monk who had been ordered to give a two hour lecture on the value of communication. Lily tried to look as if she was in the habit of organising him and then, having failed rather miserably at that particular little imitation, she settled for looking like her mother when she was putting her foot down. Gentle but firm, decided but understanding, determined but not forcible. Matt looked remarkably unimpressed. In fact his only reaction to her efforts was to stride across the room and fling open the window.

'You realise you haven't once taken me out,' said Lily plaintively.

'So? You haven't once taken me out.'

'Okay. I'm taking you out.'

'No you're not!'

Matt waved his drink at her.

'This is a man's world. Haven't you seen the advertisements?'

He couldn't understand what had got into Lily. She'd never had this lunatic desire to go out before. Before – yesterday, and all the preceding yesterdays – she'd always been perfectly content to stay in and work. That was why he liked her. She wasn't *like* all those other women he'd never bothered to take out. Lily didn't want you to become someone else so as to satisfy some feminine yearning to wear a fashionable dress, or show off a new hairstyle. She didn't pester you to go to restaurants, or insist on going to Charity Premieres like other members of her sex. Lily was nice. She looked nice, she smelt nice, and – what on earth had got into her?

'Come on – where would you like to go?'

Lily flapped her notebook at Matt.

'I've made a list. One. Walk in Hyde Park. Look at people. Feed ducks.'

'Amazing. *Very* original.'

'All right. One. Walk in Hyde Park. Look at ducks. Feed people. Two. Stroll down Portobello Road, guess the price of the rubbish, recover over a beer in a pub.'

'I don't like pubs.'

Matt pulled at his collar and took another gulp of his drink. Didn't 'like' pubs. That was the understatement of the year. He couldn't *stand* pubs. In fact a pub to him was about as inviting as going to one of his mother's buffet supper parties and being asked to give a Noel Coward recital. He could never understand this human need to crowd into places that were dirtier than your own flat and where you paid more for your drink than was conceivably honest, in order not to be able to hear a single thing someone else was saying to you. He pulled at his collar again and felt Lily looking at him, puzzled.

'I don't like pubs,' he said again.

'Why not?'

'Because!'

Lily decided to pay no attention, but to continue with her itinerary as if Matt was thrilled.

'Three. Lunch in a Bistro. Silly shop down King's Road, ending up in nice time at Craven Cottage.'

'And who the hell lives there?'

Lily stared at him. Well, not so much stared as gaped.

'Nobody *lives* there, buggalugs,' she said beginning to laugh, 'it's Fulham's home. And this afternoon it's the local derby.'

'I have an allergy to horses.'

'Horses! This is *Footers*. Fulham versus Chelsea.'

'Footers? *Footers?*'

Matt pronounced the word as if it was rabies.

'Harry Sockit. Football,' Lily went on enthusiastically.

And then she took her favourite Harry Sockit rattle from her bag and to Matt's horror swung it expertly round her head.

'Come on the Blooz!'

'Don't *do* that!'

This was a nightmare. Matt clutched at his collar for the fifth time, and vainly attempted to stem the rising tide of panic that was filling his being. This wasn't Lily, this was someone else.

'Bistros! Pubs! Shops! Football! Your plan for a day's entertainment sounds about as much fun as – as – an invitation to a beheading.'

He poured himself another drink. And then absent-mindedly picking up a piece of the ice from the bucket he started to dab his now perspiring forehead with it. Dear God. The seventeenth had to be a bad day in the stars for him. And to think that he had been in such a wonderful mood when he woke up. Looking forward to work and to seeing Lily – and working with her. As usual. Nothing untoward happening. Just him and Lily and the flat, and the work. The ideal day, in fact; and now look what was facing him – a bad dream.

'Are you okay?'

'Of course I'm okay!'

Matt resumed his position at the window and breathed in deeply.

'I'm fine. *Fine.*'

'Anybody'd think I'd suggested something outrageous.'

Matt continued to breathe in and out at the window, slowly and deeply. How could he explain to her? How could he possibly tell her?

'Is this how you treated all your other girl friends? Keeping them all cooped up here in your ivory tower?'

Matt swung round stung and in doing so spilt some of his drink on the carpet.

'Of course it is,' said Lily crisply. 'Here he sits and watches the world go by. Tick, tock, tick, tock.'

'Tick, tock, what?'

Matt scrubbed at the carpet with his handkerchief.

'Tick, tock, the sound of tempus on the fugit.'

Lily waited for him to straighten up, but he continued to

remain enthralled by the stain on the carpet, so she stood up and then bent down for her carrier bag.

'See you.'

Matt straightened up so hastily that he spilt his drink yet again.

'See me? What do you mean see me? Where are you going?'

'Out. O.U.T. T.T.F.N. spells out,' said Lily firmly.

From behind the sofa where he was yet again engaged in scrubbing the carpet, Matt heard the door close. This wasn't like Lily. This was someone else. Mind you, if it was someone else, it was typical of women. Just as you'd got used to them being one kind of person, a nice person, they went and changed everything about them that you had originally liked and admired, and you ended up with someone quite different. He threw an angry cushion at the sofa.

'Why did it have to be ME?' he muttered.

And then with great reluctance he made his way over to the front door and unhooked his coat. Underneath it was a face framed by blonde hair. It smiled at him.

'Don't forget the bread for the ducks,' said the face.

Women.

Matt hesitated on the top step outside the flats. The outside world, horrendous to him at any time, was never more fearful than at this precise moment. This precise moment in time when he was meant to be following the gay and enthusiastic Lily on this fearful expedition. He looked at her swinging her carrier bag over her shoulder and smiling encouragingly at him. If only she knew what she was doing to him.

'Come on, Matt.'

There was one last line of retreat. Matt patted his jacket pocket.

'I've forgotten my car keys.'

Once back in the flat, the search for his car keys could go on for ever, well, anyway, for quite a while. And then with luck, he could still talk her out of all this going out business.

'Don't worry. We don't need your car,' said his torturer. 'I've got wheels. I borrowed my brother's transport. Voici.'

Matt looked over to where she was standing near a very good-looking Mercedes sports car. His love of cars overcame his reluctance.

'Ah well. I have no objections to fresh air motoring.'

'Good,' said Lily briskly. 'Because it's certainly that. Come on.'

Matt started to walk towards the Mercedes and then stopped when he heard Medusa laughing behind him.

'No, not that one, my brother's only a G.P., not a Harley Street crimp. Here. This is our transport pour le jour.'

Matt turned slowly and looked at the object of her now rapt attention. She couldn't be serious. She couldn't actually mean that she was actually proposing not only to take him to pubs, and bistros, and other hell holes, but she was also seriously thinking that they would arrive at such satanic destinations on a MOTOR-BIKE. Not only a motor-bike, but a motor-bike with a side-car. Not only a motor-bike with a side-car, but a side-car of such ancient design that it would make Boadicea's chariot look positively space age.

'What is that?'

Lily looked at him from underneath the fiendish black hat and goggles she had just donned.

'A pony and trap. What do you think it is? It's a motor-bike. Brumm. Brumm. Very al fresco.'

Matt turned on his heel.

'I think I'll just go and get my car keys.'

He patted his pocket. There was a glorious sound of the familiar friendly clink.

'I've got my car keys,' he cried triumphantly.

Lily's mouth went down at the corners. She looked at him like a Matron regarding a recalcitrant patient who would not turn over for his injection.

'On a beautiful day like this,' she breathed, 'we are not driving around stuffed up in a beastly old motor car. Come on.'

With which command Matron swung her leg expertly over the saddle and started to rev up.

'This sort of machinery went out with the Perils of Pauline,' Matt moaned above the noise.

'Oh do come on,' shouted Lily. 'Where's your sang froid? Your joie de vivre?'

'Upstairs in the drink cupboard,' said Matt succinctly.

'Okay.'

Lily shrugged her shoulders.

'I'll go without you.'

She revved up again and then looked sideways at Matt under her helmet.

'All the other men I've been out with never objected.'

'What other men?'

'Get in and I'll tell you,' shouted Medusa.

Matt contemplated the hell hole that made up the inside of the side-car and wondered what had happened to his nice tidy life. Why had Mrs Grey had the 'flu that rainy day all those weeks ago. And if she'd had to have the 'flu why hadn't the Agency sent someone, anyone, rather than the blonde madcap who was currently berating him?

He squeezed himself morosely into the side-car. It smelt dimly of cheap cigarettes such as are smoked by medical students and aspiring nurses on small grants. Matt groaned audibly. The engine beside him revved with magnificent authority and then was gone, leaving behind it the most joyous peace, the most exquisite tranquility. Suddenly Lily seemed very far away, a little speck on the horizon, a dot in the distance, as well she might, for the queen of the highway, hell's only little blonde angel, had left him marooned in the road, a lone unmoving raft without steam or horsepower. A lonely figure wandering by stopped and looked at Matt.

'Lost your paddle?' he enquired tenderly.

How and why Lily somehow managed to coerce him into continuing the fearful plan she had evolved, after that very first fiasco, Matt didn't or was currently incapable of understanding. All he knew was that, having abandoned the side-car at the start of the day, he then had to follow Lily round London in his car, she herself having scorned his motor as a form of travel fit only for the middle-aged and weary.

Matt sighed to himself. Talk about weary. He was weary and it was only half past three. The sound of the music coming from his car radio was soothing, but not soothing enough to dispel the tensions, the knots the size of tennis balls that he felt throbbing in his shoulders. What a morning. What a lunch. The strain of it all. He closed his eyes. At last Schumann's 'Arabesque' was getting through to him, down, down, into the depths, or rather into the arms, of Morphus.

'Knock! Knock!'

'What? Who's that?'

Matt sat up and rubbed his eyes.

'Vera Knell.'
'Vera Knell?'
'Vera Knell you get to?'
Matt sighed and wound the window down.
'Lily.'
Lily grimaced at him through the window.
'Aren't you going to ask me in?'
'Come in,' said Matt obediently and opened the passenger door.
Lily looked at him.
'You might at least have waited till kick off,' she said with what she considered to be remarkable restraint.
Matt jingled the change in his pocket and tried to think of a good excuse for his most recent behaviour, namely running out of the football ground to the sanctity of his car before Lily's favourite team had even set toe to football.
'Seen one kick-off you've seen 'em all,' he said lamely.
Lily switched off the radio, so that she could hold Matt's attention better.
'So what now?'
Matt stared over the top of Lily's head. What he would have *liked* to have said was – wouldn't it be a good idea if they went back to the flat and perhaps did a spot of work, but even he knew that this was not the sort of suggestion that Lily in her present mood was going to jump at.
Since he didn't appear likely to reply to her question for the next millenium Lily went on, 'I suppose we *could* have yet another riveting drive around London with me on Hurricane Harry and you trolling behind in your moe?'
She sat back suddenly and sighed.
'I don't believe this is happening.'
It was Matt's turn to look incredulous.
'What's the matter? Aren't you enjoying yourself?'
'No.'
A warm flood of relief ran through Matt. He looked at her and seeing somewhere in the darkness a tiny flicker of hope he ventured to offer his suggestion.
'I know – ' he said, as if seized with a sudden flash of inspiration, ' – let's go home.'
'I don't want to go home! I want to go out!' Lily yelled.
Matt gesticulated feebly.
'You are out.'

'Out with you.'

'You are out with me. Look. You. Me. Out.'

'I want to *do* something, Matt!'

Matt sighed. He really couldn't see what she was going on about. They had already done a lot of things. Perhaps this needed pointing out to Lily. Perhaps she needed reminding about what an active morning they'd had?

'We've done a lot of things.'

He ticked off the items with his fingers.

'We've mended your brother's side-car, had a Chinese lunch – '

'Take away.'

Matt shrugged.

'Had a take away Chinese lunch which we had to eat in the car. What's so wrong with that?'

'You were driving rather fast at the time.'

Forty miles an hour, to be absolutely accurate.

'Well you said you wanted to go round Hyde Park.'

'On *foot*.'

'There was nowhere to park this side of Birmingham. You fed the ducks.'

'Throwing bread from a moving car roughly in the direction of the Round Pond is not my idea of feeding the ducks.'

Matt shook his head. He didn't like to point out to Lily that it was hardly his fault that he was allergic to feathers, any more than it was his fault that she was not a very accurate long distance duck feeder.

'Let's go home,' he pleaded again.

And then the very next second he wished he hadn't, because the blonde booper, the gay partner of yesterday, suddenly turned on him and she was no longer the blonde booper, the laughing partner, but the enemy complete with molten lava to pour about his shoulders.

'Home?' she screeched, 'oh le mot cambron! You can go home if you want to. You can go run rings if you want to! I have to take Hurricane Harry back to Tom at the Grenadier.'

'And then?'

Lily looked at him narrowly before slamming the door, and Matt could have sworn he heard teeth grinding.

'Then,' she said, 'then I shall probably demolish rather a lot of stingoes!'

Upon utterance of which Madam swung herself aboard her fiery steed, revved it up to a point that made Matt imagine it was about to compete with the latest supersonic flights and burst out of the car park on to the highway, but not before she had gestured towards Matt's windscreen in a way that did not suggest approval of Matt, his car, or anything to do with him.

'That's very rude,' Matt muttered.

And then he realised just what a feeble remark that was, being as it was made to someone who was no longer there, but was flying through the traffic at a speed that was requiring her pursuer, namely him, to break the law. Talking of which, was he not able to observe at this very minute, the pilot of the supersonic motor bike being flagged down? Ah ha, that would teach her to set off at such an immoderate pace risking life and limb, particularly his.

'This is my lucky day.'

Matt hummed somewhat tunelessly, because even watching Lily being given the once-over by a traffic cop made his stomach contract. He had a horror of uniforms. Probably because he had spent so much time in one himself at his various loathesome schools. He stopped humming gradually and stared closer at the spectacle in front of him. Whatever Lily was telling the cop was obviously heart-rending and involved him. Not only did it involve him, judging from the amount of times she had flung an indignant hand towards his car, but it involved him in a remarkably unflattering way. He knew this from the way the policeman was now walking ponderously towards him and, if he had been in any doubt, he would certainly have known it from the way Lily was now sticking her tongue out at him. Heaven help him from mad blondes.

The policeman knocked on Matt's window and, with a now completely sunken heart, he wound it down, with the intention of saying 'good evening officer' in dulcet tones, but somehow no noticeable noise escaped and instead he heard only the policeman.

'Now then, Rasputin. What's all this I hear about you pursuing and menacing innocent young ladies?'

'If you believe that, pigs have wings,' Matt snapped.

Then he slowly closed his eyes. Wrong, molto wrong, molto molto molto wrong.

At first Lily's feelings when she entered the 'Grenadier' were those of a person who had won a difficult victory. She was thrilled with herself. She had really landed Matt in it and, although she wasn't so disloyal as to spill the beans to Tom and his friends, she couldn't help laughing rather too much at most of their jokes, because the combined effect of two stingoes downed in quick succession and the memory of Matt's horrified face when he saw the traffic cop walking towards him was enough to make her feel very merry indeed. Matt had been a total spoilsport all day, about as much fun to be with as her Uncle Boris on the day his visa ran out. He *deserved* to have a bad time. Amen to that.

And then, inevitably, when no Matt appeared, and the effect of the too-swift stingoes was beginning to make her feel rather more dizzy than joyous, she began to worry. She had only the haziest of ideas about the law and, as far as she knew, there was nothing to stop the policeman locking Matt up for the night or making him pay a stupendous fine. And of course it wasn't just the question of the speed he was going, there was also the little question of the story she had spun the policeman. Supposing he had really believed that Matt had designs on her, what then? Môche, it would be only too ironic if after she had designed a day to encourage romance Matt got arrested for evil intentions. Unfortunately the irony did nothing except lower the feeling of despondency that was now convulsing her. Môche to the power of n, trust her to do everything wrong.

The pub door swung open. Lily, who had been pretending to herself that it was a matter of indifference if it did or it did not, looked up. She could have sworn she saw Matt. There, behind the old Edwardian glass, his unmistakeable outline. Yes, there he was. What on earth was he doing? He looked as if he was practising opening and shutting doors. Eventually, to her secret relief, he finally swung the door open and sat down beside a large lady who in turn was sitting precisely by the very door that Matt had been popping in and out of like a startled bird.

Lily pretended to talk very animatedly to one of Tom's friends. This was a good ruse, in her opinion, after all it would be extremely foolish if, after his recent behaviour, she showed any kind of interest in Matt's presence in the pub. In fact, now she came to think of it, and now he was here, and not in prison, she wasn't even sure that Matt's presence in the 'Grenadier' *was* of any interest to her whatsoever. She continued to make all the right noises to her current drinking companion, while keeping a close watch on Matt, but only because he was behaving so oddly. First of all he was drinking all someone else's drinks, and second of all he was waving his diary about in the air, while busily mopping his brow and talking to the large lady. If she wasn't so completely disinterested in him at that moment, Lily would have given five pounds to hear what he was saying.

'Not often one gets the chance for a really good browse through one's diary.'

Matt smiled mistily at the woman beside him. The heat was intolerable. If it wasn't for the fact that he needed to keep such a close eye on the mad blonde at the bar, who for some reason completely unknown to him was finding it necessary to have one of her drinking companions' arms round her waist, if it wasn't for this fact he would have stepped outside and stayed there, but he was afraid that she might move, or dodge away from him out of one of the other exits. He waved his diary again at the person of the opposite sex beside him.

'Yes, a lot of very interesting stuff in one's diary. Did you know for instance that the commemoration of the Holy Machabees is on the same day as racing at Chepstow? While on Saturday the third of November, the feast of St Gregory the wonder worker, there's a mixed meeting at Doncaster and Mr Beasley is coming to mend my wing chair.'

Matt knocked back another whisky, which for some reason best known to himself a large gentleman who had clearly but recently arrived from a wedding reception, kept pressing into his hands.

'Cheerz,' said the gentleman.

'Very kind,' Matt murmured.

'Sane again?' demanded the gentleman, having watched Matt throw the last order back as quickly as the first.

'Yes, yes,' Matt agreed.

The obliging gentleman departed weaving a slow but purposeful path towards the bar, while Matt continued in his deliberations.

'How are you on shortest practicable road distances? The shortest practicable road distance between Exeter and Aberdeen is 559 miles.'

Lily had got up from the bar, and coincidentally it was at that moment that Matt lost interest in the distance between Exeter and Aberdeen.

'Who wants to know the distance between Exeter and Aberdeen?' he protested. 'No wonder I never read my diary.'

Lily stopped by Matt's table.

'I say I say I say, look who it is!'

She started backwards in surprise. Not the best bit of acting she had ever done, but she thought it might convince Matt in his present condition.

'Look who what is?' he said thickly.

'I thought you were helping the police with their enquiries,' said Lily.

'Very funny. Now if you don't mind, I am just having a quiet friend with my drinks. Drink with my friends.'

'He's giving us readings from his diary,' said the large lady helpfully.

'What fun.'

'It certainly was,' said Matt defensively.

And then for want of something better to say to Lily he introduced her to his audience of one.

'This is Doris.'

'Betty.'

'This is Doris Betty. Will you kindly leave that door open!'

This last was to an innocent who had attempted to close the pub door after him. Matt patted his forehead feverishly.

'Are you all right? You look a trifle chaud.'

Lily momentarily dropped her role of Lady Indifference and leant forward to examine Matt more closely.

'Of course I'm all right,' he snapped. 'I'm fine. You don't have to worry about me.'

'Cer-come on, Lily. We'll be ler-late.'

'You remember my brother Tom, don't you?' asked Lily.

'I remember your brother Tom.'

How could he ever forget?

'How are you, brother Tom?'

'Fer-fer-fer-fer-fer-'

'Come on, Tom,' said Lily hastily.

It was fatal to ask Tom how he was.

'Fer-fer-fer-fer-fer-'

'We're all just off to a party. No point in trying to interest you I suppose?'

'I'm fer-fer-fer-fer-fer-'

'Why is there no point in trying to interest me you suppose?'

'Because it'll be full of people having fun and enjoying themselves that's why.'

'I'm fer-fer-fer-fer-fer-'

Tom turned in desperation to Lily.

'For God's sake how am I, Lily?'

'You're fine, Tom,' Lily agreed.

'I'm fer-fer-fer-fer-'

'Good. So am I, Tom,' Matt nodded.

'You don't look it,' said Tom, relieved to be off the subject of his own health. 'You look to me as if you suffer from the Ker-Ker-'

'Yes, I do,' said Matt hastily. 'I got the Ker-Ker in the Balearics and I've never been the same since.'

'So you don't want to come to the party?'

'Of course I want to come to the party. I love parties, I really do. Really. It's that I don't normally go to them that's all.'

Lily smiled at Matt for what seemed to him to be the first time for hours.

'Come on then, Ratface.'

Progress to parties on Saturday night in London usually takes a somewhat universal form, and Matt's progress to Lily's brother Tom's friend's party proved to be no exception. Far too many people got into his car, causing him to have to let down the roof. And then of course no one knew exactly where the party exactly was, except of course it was somewhere off South Kensington, but then was there ever a party given by someone's brother's friend that wasn't somewhere off South Kensington?

And even when the address was traced there was some considerable doubt about the number and which block it was in, with the result that they all had to wait until other revellers turned up, so that they could follow them in with cries of 'of course' and 'I told you it was 54B'. None of this would necessarily have counted for much with a man who was even a half-hearted party-goer, but for Matt it proved to be the long wait before the tortuous business of going up in the lift and then entering the dark brown interior that passed as their host's flat.

'Come on. Come and dance.'

Lily looked at Matt pleadingly. He was behaving so oddly, even for Matt. Refusing to move from the hall and then walking up and down as if he was a trapped tiger.

'It's all right, I'm fine. *Fine.*'

'Matt?'

Lily put a tentative hand into his.

'I wish you'd tell me what's the matter.'

'There is absolutely nothing the matter! Now go and dance. Enjoy yourself, and leave me alone.'

'Oh. Run rings.'

Matt watched her departure in total misery and then wandered over to the other side of the hall for what seemed to be the hundredth time. There was a dim light inside the cupboard that housed the coats. He pulled open the door and then shut it again, pulled it open and then shut it again, pulled it open and then shut it again. It wasn't long before he realised the secret that the cupboard was harbouring. The light was not going off! Ah ha. The wonder of modern electrics, the marvel of the era, the click switch was not clicking. His worthy host was the owner of a non-clicking click switch. He shut the cupboard again. But no, this time the light appeared to go off. To click off or not to click off? There was only one way to solve this particular mystery. Matt went into the cupboard and shut the door.

No one saw him. Least of all Lily, because she was too busy *really* enjoying herself. *Really* having a good time, dancing and laughing. And oh môche, having such a good time. But then somehow, after a while, having a good time becomes a little pointless if the person to whom you are proving you are having such a good time is not present. Lily went in search of Matt.

It had been fully an hour since anyone had seen him. She turned to Tom.

'Oh *Tom*, he has gone home and I don't blame him. He's probably gone home in a rage and I'll never ever see him again! Oh Tom!'

'Now Ler-Lily – '

'Tom, so much for cat and mouse games. I think I'll just get my coat and emigrate.'

'I'll ger-go and have a ler-last look round.'

Tom went off looking re-assuringly brotherly and dependable. Not that it would do much good. Matt had gone. She would never see him again. She opened the hall cupboard to get her coat, but instead of a neat row of coats hanging on hangers, she saw a large heap of extremely untidy overcoats flung all over the place and in the middle of them was Matt, lying as one dead, his shirt in ribbons, his tie half way round his head and himself obviously in a state of half-consciousness.

'Matt! Matt!'

Lily knelt down beside him. Matt looked at her dumbly and muttered. Lily bent closer to him to hear what he was muttering.

'The light stays on, Lily, the light stays on.'

'What light stays on?'

Matt's lips moved with difficulty.

'I only came in to see if the light stayed on.'

'What have you done to yourself, Matt? Look at your shirt.'

'The door jammed and I couldn't breathe. I couldn't breathe, Lily.'

'Oh Matt, what are you talking about?'

Lily tried not to laugh.

'The door doesn't jam – look.'

'DON'T SHUT THAT DOOR!'

'Matt – there's nothing wrong with this door. See. What on earth happened to you?'

'The door jams, Lily! I went inside and the door jams!'

'Show me what happened.'

'Right.'

They came out of the cupboard and very patiently Lily watched him re-enact the scene. He was here. Right? Right. And then he went inside and shut it. She followed him back into the cupboard. Right.

'I went inside. And shut it.'

Matt did so. Lily looked at him and then pushed the door.

'And the door jams,' she said calmly. 'Right.'

Matt grabbed first her and then the door handle.

'Help! Help! We can't breathe. Help!'

Lily took one of his hands with some difficulty.

'There's no need to panic, Matt. There's masses of air in here. Somebody'll let us out.'

'No need to panic! You don't suffer from claustrophobia!'

So that was it.

'Claustrophobia?'

A flood of relief something akin to letting unleash the waters of the Aswan Dam swept over Lily. So that was why. Football match crowds, pubs, crowds, parties, crowds. Her plan of joyous events, her list of gay happenings, would have been about as appealing to Matthew Browne Claustrophobic as the sight of sage and onion stuffing to a goose.

'Why didn't you *tell* me?'

'Because – because – '

Lily took hold of his other hand.

'Do I give you claustrophobia?'

'Of course you don't! Everybody does! It's not you, Lily. I've suffered from it all my life! It's not *you*. I can't go *anywhere*. Crowded – not that's crowded. I find it extremely difficult – going out. Or – I just find it very difficult.'

'Kiss me, Matt.'

'*Kiss* you? I can't. I can't kiss anybody without feeling I'm drowning.'

'But that's how you're *meant* to feel.'

'It isn't.'

'Of course it is.'

'No – call for help first, please. I can't breathe. I think I'm going to pass out.'

'It's all right. I know my first aid.'

'You do?'

Lily pulled Matt gently towards her and then after only a bare second or two of what turned out to be the most felicitous of experiences, she released him again. Matt's eyes opened slowly.

'I can breathe,' he whispered.

'What they call the kiss of life.'

'And I can kiss. I can. I can kiss you and I can *breathe*. I *can breathe* again, Lily.'

Lily took his dear, now for once unworried, face in her hands.

'Yes,' she said calmly, 'now I think we both can, Ratface.'

CHAPTER FIVE

Black and white and red all over

Playing in public to large audiences had proved anathema to Matt over the last fifteen years, reminding him as it did of his 'child prodigy' period, when his mother had dragged him from one large concert hall to another, until at last she had broken his spirit so completely that for a number of years even the sight of a keyboard had been enough to bring on a fit of such trembling that only a sedative could calm him. Now, however, he could once again play publicly, although only to limited audiences, such as at Antonia Lavenham's soiree.

He had finished playing when she came over and introduced herself in the sophisticated way that he always found so confusing in people.

'There is someone who is dying to talk to you.'

Matt paused in the middle of collecting his music together, and glanced at the glamorous blonde who had addressed him.

'Who?' he asked disinterestedly.

Mrs Lavenham dropped herself down beside him.

'Your hostess,' she breathed.

'You're my hostess.'

'And you're very sharp.'

Matt looked at her.

'So is your piano. It's criminal to own such a wonderful instrument and then neglect it.'

'I've been telling my husband that for years.'

'When was it last played, for crying out loud?' continued Matt indignantly.

'Ah,' she sighed.

Then she put her hand over Matt's.

'I like your touch. You must come down and entertain us at one of our little country week-ends.'

'Oh yes?'

Matt started to edge towards the door. The social whirl was about as attractive to him as spending the day at the Harrods sales with his mother.

'We have a little place in the Cotswolds,' his hostess went on. 'Tell me, are you strictly classical – or do you ever swing?'

'It depends,' Matt hedged. 'It depends where and what I'm at.'

'And what are you presently at?'

'Removing the mark from your mahogany,' he replied, buffing the Steinway with his pocket handkerchief.

'Besides removing the mark from my mahogany.'

'This and that.'

Matt shrugged. He wished she would go away. Her decollete was decidedly – well – it was decidedly something that he didn't wish to concentrate on, particularly at the moment, and not only that, her scent was so musky it was making him feel hot. He looked longingly over her shoulder to the door, beyond which lay freedom. If she would just move a little to his right he could make a bolt for it, but no such luck – she was as immoveable as the Rock of Ages.

'As a matter of fact, I'm working with someone on a musical for the stage.'

'But how *thrilling*. You must come and talk to my husband about it. He's looking for something just like that to invest in.'

'He is? Really?'

'You must come and meet him.'

Antonia took Matt's hand.

'He's an absolute powerhouse. That's him asleep over there.'

Matt sighed inwardly as he looked across at the large recumbent figure his hostess had just indicated, but then swallowing his pride he started to walk slowly after her because, as every musician knows, one must suffer to sell and, by the look of Tug Lavenham, Matt was about to suffer.

It wasn't like her mother to fuss or be possessive, but ever since Lily had confessed to her that her relationship with Matt had progressed more than somewhat – on account of the 'day out' – Mrs Pond had taken to clicking her tongue at the oddest moments, or casting anxious looks at Lily. It was all very odd and not at all like Ma. And as for this country week-end that she, Lily, was going on, well you would have thought that she had been invited to an orgy with the Hellfire Club, instead of a prim week-end at someone's rustic abode.

'I will not be needing any long-sleeved vests, Ma.'

Lily looked at the pile of vests her mother had laid carefully at the bottom of the suitcase. Her mother shook her head and clicked her tongue for the ninetieth time.

'It can be very cold in England in July, Lily. Remember that poor man who died of exposure at that regatta?'

'He was ninety-eight, Ma, and he didn't die of exposure. He died of old age.'

Mrs Pond sighed for the ninety-first time.

'Old age, exposure, you tell me the difference.'

'I am not taking any woolly underclothes, Ma,' said Lily.

Her mother looked at her. Lily had that firm but kind look that her father used to get once or twice a year and which Mrs Pond knew only too well was about as worth arguing with as it was trying to pretend it wasn't there. Mrs Pond sighed again.

'I don't know about this at all, Lily. I don't know about you going off with a member of the lunatic fringe. I don't know. What would your father have said?'

'Have a good time.'

'You just be careful with yourself.'

Lily sat down on the bed beside her mother and took one of her small, lined, overworked hands in hers.

'He's a very nice maniac musician, Ma,' she said gently. 'And even if he did have "designs" on my body, with all this vast range of invincible clothing you've packed for me, he'll never get through.'

Mrs Pond shook her head and looked at her daughter.

'Lily,' she sighed, 'the male always gets through.'

Hardly had she uttered this summary of feminine wisdom than the doorbell rang and with the eternal flurry that always seems attendant on most female departures they both started to hurry backwards and forwards, piling more and more clothes into Lily's suitcase until, with the best will in the world, neither of them was able to shut the case, not even when they both bounced up and down on it with full force. The situation quite obviously called for a man and, since Matt had just arrived, Mrs Pond could see that it would be impractical not to call on his services as a case shutter, even thought it was against her principles to let a man into the bedroom of a single girl of unblemished virtue, such as she ardently hoped her daughter to be.

Matt was summoned. And quite relieved to be summoned he was too, having just finished the stickiest five minutes of an already extremely sticky relationship with Lily's grandmother. Quite apart from sniffing every so often and making icy remarks about 'strolling bandoliers' who took innocent girls on lurid week-ends. Lily's grandmother was fine, just fine. Matt hurried quickly towards the room where Lily was calling to him, only to be passed in the corridor by a lady who looked the right age to be Lily's mother, but who flung a look at him as if he was a wolf that had just eaten up grandmama and then hurried silently on. By the time he reached Lily and her room, Matt was convinced that there was something about him that his best friend – if he'd had one – hadn't told him. He was just about to ask Lily the fifty thousand dollar question when he caught sight of her suitcase.

'What is all this? You will not be needing all these clothes for one week-end!'

Lily looked at Matt resignedly. Honestly, typical Matt, not even a hallo-how-are-you-don't-you-look-nice-and-how-nice-to-meet-your-family. Oh no, straight into the stream of invective and the wild hand being waved frenetically under her nose.

'You will not be needing all these clothes for one week-end,' he repeated more gently.

'Won't I?'

'No. They are *Londoners*, Lily. And they have a week-end retreat. You know the sort of thing. All rush matting and converted oil lamps. So précis the packing, Miss Pond. We have to leave in a minute.'

Lily looked from Matt to her suitcases and back again to Matt. All those frantic arguments with Ma, all for nothing. All those 'Have you got the right bra for that dress' conversations and 'won't you be needing four pairs of tights in case you go beagling?' All to no avail.

'Oh môche,' she said sadly, 'I was rather looking forward to sweeping down the grand stairs in my moulded chiffon.'

Matt shook his head. Really, women had the oddest

ideas of what went on in the country. Moulded chiffon indeed – the most she'd need would be a pair of wellington boots for a walk after Sunday lunch.

All the way down to Manor Lodge, the Lavenham's country cottage, Lily kept exclaiming, 'Look Matt cows', or 'look Matt green fields', until Matt, who had started off the journey in pretty bad shape, on account of the quite awful business of having to help Lily unpack under Mrs Pond's wrathful eye, was forced to allow himself to relax. There was something about Lily's enthusiasm about every single incident to do with the journey that got through to you. Like the Mole in *Wind in the Willows* out on his first picnic, she seemed prepared to enjoy everything and anything, even down to getting out and operating the self-service machine at the petrol station. And although her map reading was about as parlous as her shorthand she did eventually manage to steer them in the right direction, viz Little Compton Under Ashfold, a pretty Cotswold village entirely in keeping with the rush matting and converted oil lamps image.

'This is it all right.'

Matt nodded sagely. Never the safest driver at the best time, he felt considerable relief at having reached their destination without accident and with only the cottage itself to find.

'Now just remember, we are here to fish for backing for our musical, so don't go doing or saying anything too outrageous. We need all the support we can get.'

Lily finished combing her hair and nodded nervously. Whatever she did she did not wish to let Matt down. Not ever, ever.

'Now keep your eyes peeled for the typical trendy week-end conversion. Two up and two down and a colour television aerial.'

Lily nodded again and stared obediently out of the window.

'What's the place called?'

'Manor Lodge,' said Matt, 'it's somewhere on the left, according to Mrs Lavenham's instructions.'

They passed a large house complete with sweeping drive, and sweeping lawns. Matt nodded wisely.

'That's obviously the manor so I take it Manor Lodge

can't be too far from it. What does it say on the gate?'

Lily got out and went and peered at the elegant gates bearing the name of the house. She came back to report.

'Well?'

'You're not going to like this, Ikey – but *this* is Manor Lodge.'

'This can't be the place.'

'Oh yes dis is, Massa – hundred and two up and a hundred and two down – and no sign of a television aerial. What did you say about fishing? I've a feeling it's us that's been caught.'

They drove up the drive with mutually sinking hearts. Lily thinking of the wardrobe she had left behind on her bed at Streatham, a wardrobe that would go only too well with the thirty-five stairs that led up to the portico, and not too badly with the Filippino butler that was hurrying down to meet them. Oi vai, she could just imagine what was going to happen when she came down to dinner in her neatly pressed Levis and her wellies. She hadn't got time to be rude to Matt, most unfortunately, because the butler had just opened the car door for her.

In fact they were both half way up the steps to the front door, if you could call the magnificent portico by such a pedestrian name, when Lily, to her immense relief, realised that she had forgotten her bag.

'I've left my bag,' she said to Matt. 'You go on.'

Matt, who was fully aware of the kind of invective that would be waiting for him from his steely eyed partner, could only nod briefly at her departing figure and hope she wouldn't abscond with his car. To be left alone to dress for dinner in a place that more than slightly resembled Blenheim Palace with only a pair of jeans and your wellies for apparel was about as appetising to Lily as it would be to most members of the opposite sex, and who could blame her? Why did he have to go and make her unpack? Oh why, oh why was he alive at all? Which was a good question, but he had no time to answer it since here was their hostess.

'Matthew. Dear Matthew.'

'Mrs Lavenham.'

'Antonia. So you left your boring old partner behind after all?'

'Er. No – my boring old partner's getting something from the boring old car.'

'Oh. Do come in.'

Matt entered a hall that was so large that at first he had difficulty taking it all in. And then when he had he realised that it was not only a hall, but a hall cum sitting room, and that it was furnished even on this quite warm day with a log fire burning, complete with two English setters, and a recumbent sleeping figure that he recognised as being that of Mr Lavenham – host.

'So,' Antonia looked at him roguishly. 'So you found it all right?'

'No.'

Matt attempted a joke.

'We found it all wrong.'

'Oh.'

Antonia tinkled a laugh.

'Oh,' she said again.

There was a silence and then Matt, who was beginning to feel that he was about to melt, said vaguely, 'Cold isn't it?' and tugged at his collar, wishing for the now twentieth time that he was back at his piano in his flat getting really stuck on his newest composition. Anything was preferable to this.

'Isn't it *boring*?' asked Antonia, out of nowhere. Then before Matt could think of a reply, she said, 'God I do so hate the country, it's so boring. Tug loves it of course, don't you, Tug?'

She kicked the bottom of Mr Lavenham's country encrusted boots.

'Uh? That's it. On we go,' muttered Tug and fell back asleep again.

'Anyway, I'm so glad you could make it. Oh,' Antonia turned, 'who's that at the door?'

'Yes.'

Matt hurried over to Lily.

'Yes, this is my boring old partner.'

Hardly had the words floated from his mouth when he realised that he had managed to bring off a double. Both Lily and Antonia were staring first at him, and then at each other, with about as much delight as a someone who has just been presented with yesterday's fish as a birthday present.

'Oh,' said Antonia.

Lily said nothing, and before her silence could deepen into open hostility, Ning Ning, the Filippino Jeeves appeared and led Matt up to his room, a fairly exhausting business, not because he Matt was carrying the suitcases, but because the staircase was obviously not designed by someone who had taken 'moderation in all things' to be his motto.

Matt looked round his room. It wasn't too large, in fact if it were to try and pass as a State Room on a luxury liner it would probably be considered small.

'Nothing too elaborate. Ha, ha.'

Matt sat down heavily on the fourposter bed. A minute of reverie was followed by a knock at the door.

'Who is it?'

Lily's voice floated towards him.

'Cantwee.'

Matt sighed.

'Cantwee who?'

'Cantwee please go home?'

'No we can not go home!' said Matt sharply. 'These people are very interested in what we're doing.'

Lily looked at him morosely.

'They haven't seen my wellies yet.'

'Will you just leave all this to me. You know nothing about this side of the business. We have to chat these people up.'

'So what are we meant to wear for dinner, Matt?'

This long anticipated cry was interrupted by another very welcome knock.

'Yes?'

It must have been the fact that he had observed the Oriental custom of crossing his palm with silver that had done it, because in came Ning Ning with a large silver bowl bearing what looked like really appetising and exquisite fruits.

'It's getting more Upstairs Downstairs by the minute,' muttered Lily.

'S'll right, Boss?'

Matt nodded.

'Yes thank you. Everything's fine.'

Lily dropped her voice and surreptitiously kicked Matt on a tender part of his shin.

'Ask him, ask Confucious what to wear.'

'No,' said Matt stubbornly. 'Oh all right – excuse me.'

'Ah so Boss?'

Ning Ning beamed expectantly.

'Dinner. What we wear for dinner?'

'So?'

The message was not getting through. Matt did an elaborate eating mime.

'So?'

'Look.'

Matt pointed at Lily's jeans.

'Jeans? Can we wear jeans?'

'Heans?' asked Ning Ning hesitantly.

'No *jeans,*' corrected Matt.

'No jeans,' repeated Ning Ning.

'Yes, no jeans?'

'Yes, no jeans,' agreed Ning Ning obediently.

'You mean – not jeans, black tie?' asked Matt with a heavy heart.

'Ack lie?' questioned Ning Ning.

'Black tie,' corrected Matt.

'Ah so Boss, *Lack tie.*'

'Black tie, yes?'

'Lack tie, yes?'

'Lack tie, yes, lack tie yes,' murmured Ning Ning happily and departed leaving Matt to sink once more back on to the four poster, and Lily's mouth to turn down at the corners like a child's drawing.

'Let's go home,' she moaned.

'We will not go home. And will you just leave all this to me?'

Matt walked up and down the vast bedroom once or twice, while Lily watched him expectantly. After a moment or two since he didn't seem to be exactly spouting good ideas, or waving a magic wand and turning her wellies into glass slippers, she went to one of the cupboards.

'Eureka! Look Matt!'

'Now what? The remains of yet another underpacked guest?'

'Crumbs from a rich man's table.'

Lily waved her hand at a vast row of dresses and suits, quite obviously put away pending the annual Christmas bazaar. Lily took out an aged dinner suit for Matt and took an equally aged evening dress down and held it up against herself.

'Ready when you are Mr de Mille,' she said and flew off to change.

In fact once on, the dress fitted her fairly well, here and there, and where it didn't, she wasn't prepared to complain, because after all, when all was said and done, crumbs from a rich man's table were crumbs, and it would be extremely greedy to expect fairy tales to come true, and for everything including the borrowed evening gloves to be totally perfect. Any more than it would be optimistic to the point of madness to expect Matt to be looking comfortable in an aged dinner jacket, and very worn bow tie. When you had just been thrown some manna from heaven there was no point in complaining that you didn't like the taste.

Obviously Matt felt as she did because neither of them commented on the appearance of the other, but set off in the direction of the main hall, waddling along like two old ducks, because the Lavenham's old clothes were as long in the hem as they were obviously long in the teeth. The increasing murmur of people passing the time of day while drinking gin and tonics and eating peanuts floated up from the hall towards them. Matt adjusted his stringy bow tie nervously. Lily took his arm and squeezed it.

'Courage mon brave,' she whispered, and then they both rounded the corner in the stairs and confronted the downstairs gathering.

Below them stood a large room well furnished with people in every form of clothing except evening dress. Lily's grip on Matt's arm tightened as they started to make the horrifying descent towards their casually dressed fellow guests. There was very little that could be said at this particular juncture of the proceedings, but as the faces of the assembled company grew nearer, and the expression of amazement with them, Lily turned to Matt.

'What is black and white and red all over?'

'I don't know. Tell me. What is black and white and red all over?'

Lily smiled sweetly at him.

'Well don't look now, buster, but've a feeling it's us – blush, blush?'

Happily enough the worst part of any evening when you dress wrong is the entrance. Once the full shock of how wrong you've gone dawns on you and your fellow guests, there really is nothing more to be done except scramble through the evening as best you can, and hope that the time for you to make your departure will arrive so sensationally quickly that you will be pleasantly surprised.

Unfortunately for Lily, who had survived the dinner in spite of sitting next to a man who blew down his nostrils at her like a horse on a frosty morning and equally in spite of the looks that Tug Lavenham kept throwing at her decollete, the aftermath of the dinner proved to be even more boring than the dinner itself. 'Leaving the gentlemen with the port' wasn't something that you did a lot of in Streatham, and by the time Lily had concealed her ninth yawn she was jolly glad that she came from Streatham and not Ashburton under Wychwood, or wherever they were. Ladies together were not exactly stimulating. Women do not like each other, they do not even pretend to like each other, in fact the most women will do is to reluctantly acknowledge each other's existence, the way that dogs pass each other with hackles raised.

'So.'

Antonia broke the endless silence that had lapped about them for the preceding minutes.

'So.'

'So,' echoed the lady on the sofa.

And then possibly to try and drown the distant noise of all those men enjoying themselves, she said disinterestedly, 'What's your Penelope up to, Tonia? Still at nursery school?'

'No, she's just got divorced actually.'

Antonia blew a perfect smoke ring and watched it float towards the chimney piece.

'Gawd, don't they grow up *so* quickly nowadays?'

'It depends what you put on them,' said Lily.

The woman on the sofa stared at her.

'God the country's so boring,' sighed Antonia to no one in particular.

There was another roar from the direction of the dining room. Evidently the gentlemen didn't share Antonia's sentiments.

'What on earth are they up to now, Tonia?'

'Oh probably throwing buns at The Stag at Bay, or peeing in the wine coolers.'

'Your Saturdays are such fun, so civilised,' someone echoed from behind the coffee pot.

Antonia sighed.

'God the country's so boring,' she said again and they all fell once more to contemplating the enormity of this truth.

It was saying something for the liveliness of the assembled company that they all managed to sit up and look pleased when Tug and his cohort of merry men deigned to join the ladies.

'Percy got the bugger right between the antlers. Bloody fine shot.'

'Ah, there you are, Tug, now perhaps we can all have a swipe. Our tongues are hanging down to our knees.'

'On we go, on we go,' agreed Tug.

Then he leant towards Lily and murmured, 'Damn nice piece of frock that, Lily.'

His companion agreed heartily.

'Damn nice. Wish to Gawd old Geraldine would wear something like that. Instead of all this pouffy nonsense. One shopping trip down the King's Road and she comes home thinking she's solved the Generation Gap.'

'Want a swipe, Lily?' asked Tug.

He held up two bottles.

'Some of this green muck or some of this brown muck?'

'Some of the green muck would be terrific, thank you.'

Over Tug's shoulder Lily could see Matt weaving his way unsteadily into the centre of the room.

'Scusi,' she murmured. 'Won't be a tic.'

And she hurried over to Matt.

'Are you all right?'

'I am,' said Matt, 'amazingly all ride. Amazingly.'

'Your mouth's gone all red.'

Matt gave her a dazzling smile that stopped a little too abruptly and then appeared to slide down the side of his face and into his collar.

'What are you doing with me?' he went on. 'You are meant to be chadding up mine host. Money, money, money. Your job is to chad up Mr Moneybags.'

Hardly had he said this when Mrs Antonia Moneybags came floating across to them, closely followed by the previously mentioned Mr Tug Moneybags.

'Matthew, *dear* Matthew. Do come and tell us what is scandalising the musical world.'

'On we go, on we go,' muttered Tug.

He smiled at Lily while pouring far too much brandy into Matt's far too eager glass.

'Thank you very much,' said Matt over-gratefully.

'Matt,' whispered Lily. 'Be careful.'

'I'm fine, I'm fine,' said Matt bravely.

'Got to keep going old thing,' agreed Tug approvingly.

And at the same time as Antonia slipped her arm gracefully through Matt's, Tug did the same to Lily, leaving little room for argument. The attack and ambush was entire Lavenham victory. Lily sighed. It was obviously going to be a long, long evening.

Being right isn't much fun when you don't want to be, at least Lily didn't think so. She had been so right about the length of the evening that hers could have qualified as one of the Great Predictions of Our Century. First of all she had to sit through Matt singing every George Gershwin number he had never learnt properly, and then she'd had to sit and pretend to be riveted by Tug's mutterings while catching the drift of Matt's equally unimpressive conversation with the ladies. And now here they were still up, and still going strong, at half past two, if you can call listening to a drunken pianist and staring into the dying embers of a fire 'going strong'.

'Wasn't that terrific?' Antonia asked the snoring Tug, and the bored Lily, as Matt finished yet another hideous rendition of 'Pennies from Heaven'.

'Terrific,' murmured Lily.

'You're such a clever boy.'

Antonia poured Matt another brandy.

Matt smiled at her.

'I doan thin I wan any more to drin. K.'

Antonia pulled him up from the piano stool.

'Now they've all gone home you must come and sit here, and tell me all about your show while – er – Lily goes on chatting to Tug.'

She patted the cushion beside her, and pulled the compliant Matt down beside her. And then because even she couldn't ignore Tug's loud snores, she hurled a cushion in his direction.

'Tug, wake up, and get off your bum and show Lily the Conservatory.'

'Supposing Lily doesn't want to see the Conservatory?'

'Of corze Libby doez,' said Matt.

'Of course Lily does,' agreed Antonia. 'Tug's got the most famous philodendron in the Cotswolds.'

Tug wobbled obediently to his feet.

'Got to keep going,' he murmured, 'got to keep going. On we go, on we go.'

'Matt.'

Lily looked across at Matt pleadingly.

Antonia interrupted her quickly.

'Matt can tell me all about your little venture,' she said sweetly.

Lily followed the muttering Tug out of the room and then, because she trusted Antonia just about as much as a fork-tongued adder, she left Tug to wander off drunkenly to the Conservatory and stayed to watch the ensuing scene between mine hostess and their mutual composer friend.

'So.'

She smiled at Matt, a smile that was completely wasted as it happened, because Matt appeared to be concentrating very hard on something on the ceiling.

'I think it's time we were in bed,' she said softly.

This statement had the desired effect of making Matt take his gaze down from the ceiling and address her with some passion.

'No you muzzn go to beb! Nod until I've thralled you wid my talent and cabtivaded you with my charb.'

'But I am captivated. And that's why I think we should go to bed.'

'See. I am borin you.'

'You are not boring me.'

'Bud you wan to go to beb.'

'Of course I want to go to bed.'

Antonia smiled softly.

'Ride!'

Matt nodded morosely.

'Ride. Then we must *all* go to beb.'

He drew himself with some difficulty to his feet and then

staggered towards the stairs, closely followed by Antonia, who, true to type, was smiling in a way that Lily could just imagine a viper would smile before swallowing his breakfast. Lily waited until they had disappeared out of sight and then she too followed them up the stairs. It was obviously going to be all hands on deck time for rabbit lovers.

Antonia had disappeared into Matt's room by the time Lily arrived up outside his door, but she could hear him still carrying on, while Antonia too was obviously also carrying on, but not quite in such a verbose way as Matt.

'All ardisds. All ardisda everywhere deave or alide. Dead or alive bud particularly dead have always. Always. Haven't they? Needed *encouragement.*'

'I shall give you encouragement,' murmured Antonia.

'Then thad is wunnderful. Wunnerful! Whad are you doing?'

'Taking off your clothes.'

'That is wunnerful. Whad wood all ardisds have other done everwise? Look at Vinzen Van. And Rembran. Do you know people are more interested in his stupid ear than whad he ever paided?'

'Of course they are,' Antonia agreed silkily.

At which point Lily decided that she'd eavesdropped quite enough to know what the scene was. She knocked loudly on the door.

There was a chorus of 'ssssshhhs', and then silence. And then quite suddenly Matt's voice shouted, 'Who is it?'

'Matt! Matt! It's me,' called Lily.

'Iz her,' Lily heard him say to Antonia.

'Whom?' he added after some thought.

'Lily,' said Lily.

The whole room suddenly appeared to erupt.

'Liddy! Id's Liddy. I didn't know Liddy was coming!'

He threw open the door and revealed himself to Lily's startled gaze to be half-naked.

'Are you all right?'

Matt sat down extremely suddenly on the bed that Antonia had obviously been aiming him for.

'I am azinly all ride,' he announced to both women.

Antonia 'smiled' at Lily.

'Just making sure Matthew had everything he wanted.'

'Terrific,' said Lily crisply.

'So.'

'*Goodnight,*' said Lily.

'Goodnight.'

Matt was still intent on giving his lecture on artistic needs to whoever should be mad enough to listen.

'I mean shud we all be odderwise? Any of us?' he asked Lily finally.

'You should be in bed.'

'I second thad.'

'But not in here.'

Lily pulled him to his feet.

'This isn't where you're sleeping.'

'Of corse it's where I'm – gosh you're preddy.'

'No I'm not.'

Lily pushed him to his swaying feet.

'And your room for tonight is across the corridor – in my room.'

'But,' Matt protested vigorously 'bud what is to become os uf? Of us? Gosh you're preddy. Very preddy. Whad is to become os uz?'

'You are going to go to bed that's what is to become of you.'

Lily gave him a final shove into her room and shut the door. Three seconds later it re-opened.

'Gosh you're preddy,' murmured Matt.

But Lily stuffed him back into her room again. There was no time for that kind of talk Inspector. She had to hurry before the viper came back for her prey.

Sure enough not many minutes later there was a small scratch at the door.

'Matthew? Matthew?'

'Yes?' whispered Lily.

'It's *me,*' whispered Antonia back.

She opened the door just as Lily switched on the bedside light.

'It's me?'

'Oh,' hissed Antonia.

And then again as she took in the lump in the bed that Lily had hurriedly shaped to look like Matt.

'Oh.'

'Sssh,' said Lily.

And it was her turn this time to be 'sweet'.

‘Matt’s asleep.’

‘Oh, just popped by to see if he had everything he needed.’

‘Thank you,’ said Lily. ‘He’s got everything he needs. Goodnight.’

‘Good-bye.’

Needless to say Lily and Matt found a note on the breakfast table the next morning asking them to be so kind as to leave after breakfast, and needless to say what with one thing and another, neither of them felt much like breakfast so it wasn’t very long before they were both on their way back to London complete with wellies.

‘Hope you enjoyed your stay. Sorry it had to be so brief.’

Lily threw Antonia’s note into one of the shrubs as the car crept back down the drive again.

‘So – ’ she looked at Matt, ‘no money.’

Matt made a hungover noise that sounded rather like ‘ugh’ pronounced ‘ug’.

‘I don’t think mine host took defeat too well,’ said Lily chattily.

‘What happened exactly?’

Matt swerved to avoid a motorcyclist.

‘Boy racer!’

‘Don’t you remember anything at all?’

‘Not a thing.’

‘Ah well, then hold on to yourself Signor Matt while I tell you – ’

Matt nodded.

‘Well,’ Lily began.

And then she looked at him. He did have the most frightful hangover.

‘Well what happened was – you made me sleep in *your* room and you slept in mine, because it was perfectly obvious from the word go – so you said – what Tug was after. And when he came to get it he got you instead, and you sent him packing.’

‘I did?’

Matt turned and looked at Lily.

‘You certainly did, Ratface.’

Matt shook his head.

‘Yes, well, next time perhaps you’ll just leave everything

to *me*? You see that was the big mistake, letting you get involved.'

He shook his head again.

'Honestly, women.'

'Women,' agreed Lily happily.

There was a contented silence, while Matt contemplated his reported heroics of last night and Lily gazed out of the window. Then Lily said, 'Look Matt – horses. Look Matt – lambs.'

And on we go, as Tug would have said.

CHAPTER SIX

Mrs Browne came to Town

It had been a long time since Matt had seen Lily's brother Doctor Tom and, now that he was here, he wasn't altogether sure that he wasn't 'de trop', if not completely superfluous. After all when a man is in love he has very little need of anyone, let alone his future brother-in-law.

Tom straightened up and frowned at Matt.

'Can't imagine why Ler-Lily wanted me to have a look at you.'

Matt leapt up from his bed and grabbed his pyjama jacket.

'Perhaps she thought it might inspire you to catch a glimpse of the perfect body. The body that defies description.'

He flexed his muscles at Tom.

'You too can have a body like twine.'

Tom put away his stethoscope. In some ways he could see what Lily meant about Matt having gone peculiar, because this definitely was not the maddened composer that he had first met, nor was it the stricken individual sitting with sweat pouring down him at the 'Grenadier'. This was a gay blade, a man of carefree heart, humming 'I've got the world on a string . . . ' and bouncing about his bedroom as if he had just inherited a million dollars from an ageing aunt.

'I'm ber-beginning to see why Ler-Lily thought you weren't yourself.'

'Of course I'm not myself. And what's it because of? It's because of your sister. And why's it because of your sister? Because your sister and I are in – '

He drew a heart dramatically in the air in front of Tom.

'There is absolutely nothing physically wrong with me. I am in A.1 condition.'

'I think,' said Tom carefully, 'I ther-think it's mer-more your mental condition that Lily's worried about.'

'*About* which Lily is worried, Tom. About which. "I before E except after C". '

'Yes.'

Tom nodded and then gently posed the question which no doctor likes to ask, except when absolutely necessary.

'Is there any er-incidence of mer-mental disturbance in your family?'

Matt stopped and turned a fierce gaze upon Tom.

'Oh, now why did you have to go and bring my family up? On a lovely day like this what made you mention my *family*? Didn't anybody tell you? My family are unspeakable. Nobody speaks about my family. Not even my family. They are all so unspeakable not even my family can speak about themselves. I am about the only normal member of the entire tribe!'

'Wher-why are you putting on a ter-tie?'

'Because – Doctor – I have to go out.'

'In your per-pyjamas? You der-don't wear a tie with per-pyjamas.'

'Of course you do not wear a tie with pyjamas! I was just testing you.'

Matt ripped off his pyjama jacket and threw it carelessly across the bed, so that it landed on the bedside lamp.

'Oh – ' he said leaning conspiratorially across to Tom. 'If that person – known for some reason as my mother – even knew I was going out with your sister, let alone – '

He drew another dramatic heart in the air.

'Let alone being madly in – you're right it's too hot for a tie.'

'What's your mer-mother got to do with it?'

'Everything. This place. All this belongs to the family trust. *I* belong to the family trust. And the family trust is controlled by my mother. My father – very wisely in my opinion – upped and left her one rainy bank holiday and was last heard of running a seaman's mission in Bolivia. And as for women.'

Matt stopped brushing his hair for a second and gazed at himself soulfully in the mirror.

'As for women. If I tried to marry without the consent of the trust, all this – '

He gestured around the flat.

'All this goes. Which would not be fair on Lily. You know women, Tom. The one thing they like is to be brought up in the luxury to which they're totally unaccustomed.'

'Not Ler-Lily,' said Tom loyally. 'Lil's not a bit like that. She wer-wouldn't mind.'

'*She* wouldn't but I would, Tom. For Lily's sake I would. So, that's that.'

Quite suddenly he climbed into bed, and pulled the bedclothes up to his chin.

'I thought you were going out?' said Tom.

'I am,' agreed Matt, 'in a minute.'

Tom left him smiling serenely at the ceiling. He'd heard of people acting strangely when in love, but he had to admit in his short medical career he had never actually witnessed it and, now that he had, he had a good mind to go home and write up the obviously very acute symptoms that Cupiditis brought on. Singing, jumping about, abandoning normal habits – such as tidiness – in favour of more abnormal ones – like smiling and laughing. And then of course, last but not least, symptom number four – an inability to discard pyjamas, or leave the bed. He shook his head and waited for Lily to finish her phone call.

Lily put down the telephone.

'Well?'

'You'll be glad to hear there is absolutely ner-nothing wrong with him, as far as I can ter-tell.'

'Are you sure?'

Lily frowned.

'He's been behaving very strangely recently. I'm sure he's gone soft in the head.'

Hardly had she said this when the bedroom door flew open again and the maniacal looking Matt appeared, his pyjama jacket still clinging to him and his hair in a complete state of disarray. This Wagnerian apparition started back when it caught sight of the object of its worship, namely Lily, and breathed her name.

'Lily.'

Lily looked from Tom to Matt and back again.

'See what I mean? He has gone soft in the head.'

'Lily. Lily. Lily. Lily. Lily.'

'Okay, I'm a person not a plant catalogue.'

'You've arrived Lily. She's arrived Tom. Lily has *arrived.* Now the day may commence.'

'Then why are you still in your pyjamas? It's terrifically late and we're meant to be at work.'

'I am still in my pyjamas because I'm going out,' said Matt with commanding logic.

'In pyjamas?'

'Why not? Caesar ruled an empire in a frock. Besides I have to go and post this – at the Post Office.'

'Good choice.'

'And on the way back I shall buy you some roses and us some champagne.'

'See what I mean, Doctor?'

Lily turned to Tom.

'This is not the tyrant to whom anything but work spells distraction.'

Tom was just about to agree that the metamorphosis did seem startling in the extreme, when the gay troubadour, the laughing, singing, utterly transformed Matt, interrupted him with yet another eulogy to Lily.

'How perfect your grammar! How perfect is your smile! How perfect your frame! But most of all how sublime is your syntax! I shall return festooned with flowers and armed with French nectar –

"That I might drink and leave the world unseen,
And with thee fade into the forest dim." '

Either Lily was not in a romantic frame of mind, or else she was so used to this form of address that it now left her unmoved, because she merely nodded briskly at Matt and started to tidy up.

'Then you'd better get a move on, Shelley.'

'*Keats*,' said Matt crossly.

'And I love you too.'

Lily picked up the telephone message pad and waved it at him.

'By the way – someone's just telephoned to say they'd be popping round any minute. That singer who keeps ringing.'

Matt frowned.

'What singer who keeps . . . not – '

'Yes – Maria Bellcanto?'

Matt appeared to erupt in front of Tom and Lily's eyes.

'Maria Bellcanto? Maria Bell*canto*? She's coming round here? She's coming round *here*? She's not coming round here. She's not coming round here. Maria Bellcanto. Coming round here? Maria Bellcanto's not coming round here.'

'From the sound of it,' said Lily patiently, 'Maria Bellcanto is not coming round here.'

'She most certainly is not! The woman is a libertine. A raving nymphomaniac!'

'Oh dear, shall I leave for Australia now?'

'You are not going anywhere, I need all the cover I can get.'

'You wer-won't need me,' said Tom hastily. 'Nothing mer-much a per-plain G.P. can do for cases like that. Ner-nothing much anybody can do.'

Lily was just about to agree, when a sudden thought struck her.

'Yes there is! Running water! If you're ever trapped by a sex maniac you should keep the water running. It puts them off. I read it once in one of those funny magazines you buy on railway stations.' She turned to Matt. 'You'd better go on Matt if you're going. Then you'll be back sooner. Go on – shoo! I'll go and change into "the dressing gown".'

And then as she pushed Matt towards the front door, by way of explanation she said to Tom, 'I always wear his dressing gown when we're working, otherwise he gets distracted.'

'I see,' said Tom, who didn't at all.

'You just watch out for Maria Bellcanto,' warned Matt. 'And ker-keep the water running.'

Lily sighed.

'She's hardly going to ravage *me*, Matt.'

'She's a very funny lady,' said Matt warningly.

Lily said 'yes, yes' and shut the door after them. Honestly – talk about girls, men took much more time to say nothing than girls could possibly. She scampered off to change into Matt's dressing gown. On such a lovely morning, she couldn't wait to start work.

At just the time that Lily was scampering into Matt's bedroom and unhooking his dressing gown, Harold the porter was downstairs in his cubby hole being riveted by page three of the *Sun*. Not that page three contained the Sports Page, or last night's greyhound results, but what it did contain was sporty enough to hold Harold's attention in spite of an extremely smartly dressed lady calling 'Porter!' at him several times. Harold gently lowered his paper.

'Yes?'

The lady in question gave him a look that would have sunk more than a thousand ships. Harold rose slowly to his feet and straightened his hat.

'Yes?' he repeated, slightly less belligerently.

'Better. Not good, but better. Tell me, is Mr Matthew Browne in residence?'

Harold picked up the house phone.

'He is, Madam. Who shall I say it is?'

'His mother. But no – on second thoughts I think I would like to surprise him.'

'Shall I call the lift for you, Madam?'

Mrs Browne turned and looked at him from the bottom of the stairs.

'The *lift*?' she demanded. 'For four floors?'

Not knowing quite how to reply to this, Harold remained on his feet until she was out of sight and then returned thankfully to page three of the *Sun*, and his subsequent concentration on the picture of Miss Angie Hayes relaxing in her father's garden in Hendon was so complete that he failed to notice Mr Matthew Browne and Dr Tom Pond walking through the lobby to the outside world. But then a girl with a thirty-eight inch bust, who listed scuba diving and stock car racing as her hobbies, quite obviously deserved a second glance, a fact which although it might not alter the course of the world was certainly about to complicate Lily's morning.

'Oh môche!'

Lily wished she hadn't just heard the doorbell and knew she had.

'I bet that'll be our sexy soprano.'

She paused on her way to the front door. Matt's phrase 'She's A Very Funny Lady' flashed across her mind. It might, given that life had a habit of springing surprises on the unwary, it might be quite a good idea to turn on the shower, just in case she *was* acey deucy. After all nowadays you couldn't be too careful.

The doorbell rang again.

'All right. Coming!'

She opened the front door. Outside stood a redoubtable lady in a hat that totally resembled the Chelsea Flower Show on Fellows Day only.

'Hello?' said Lily hopefully.

'I think I rang the wrong bell,' breathed the dragon from without.

'Who are you looking for?' asked Lily.

And then in deference to Matt's compliments to her syntax, hastily changed to 'For whom are you looking?'

'Matthew Browne.'

'Then you rang the right bell.'

Lily opened the door wider.

'Is he in?'

'No – he's in his pyjamas. That is he's just popped out.'

'In his *pyjamas*? With *his* chest?'

'Yes – and with his legs and the rest of his body.'

Lily pulled Matt's dressing gown more tightly round her. She didn't know why, but she didn't like the look of this operatic woman. She had that wild starey look that she'd always been given to believe went with ladies who liked their own sex more than the opposite one.

'Do come in – ' she said, in an effort to be polite, and then ruined the whole effect by adding quickly, 'Just a bit, that's far enough.'

'And who exactly are *you*?'

She of the wild staring eyes looked Lily up and down. Bare legs, dressing gown that didn't do up properly. Oi vai.

'You're not interested in me,' squeaked Lily.

'On the contrary, I'm *very* interested in you, my dear,' growled The Hat, advancing further into the room.

'No you're not, I'm just boring old Lily. And I'm not a bit interested in sex – I mean – just pretend I'm not here. Okay.'

She attempted a smile.

'Sorry about le dressing gown – no – don't move. You'll be very comfortable there. That's the nicest part of the room. It catches all the sun. Yes, sorry about the dressing gown, but I was just getting ready for Matt. For work. For matting my work. Working with Matt. I'm making a rug. And I always get undressed for working with Matt – for working with Matt in his dressing gown. But then you don't want to hear about boring old me. Tell me all about boring old you. What do you think of the water? The weather?'

'It appears from where I am standing that you have nothing on under that dressing gown.'

'Yes I have! Yes I have! Haven't I? No I haven't! Of course I haven't because I am just about to have a bath. Can't you hear the water? Psst, psst?'

'Come here,' growled Horrid Person patting the seat. 'I want to know exactly what's going on here.'

Lily looked at her hand patting the sofa. Quel jam. Why hadn't she listened to Matt and not answered the door, or whatever it was he had been going on about not doing?

'Nothing is going on and I *must* have a bath. You know best friends not telling you and all that jive. Not you – me. I mean, posh,' she lifted up one of her arms and pumped it up and down, 'you wouldn't like me at all,' she said desperately. 'Talk about shepherd's pie, zowee!'

And she flew into the bathroom and slammed the door.

Mrs Brown stared after her. It was a nightmare. Coming to her pied à terre in London, expecting to find dear Matthew and instead the door being opened by a slut wearing her son's dressing gown and talking utter tosh.

'Matthew? Matthew?'

She peered into the bedroom. Good God it looked as if it had just witnessed a five day orgy. Shirts all over the lamps, ties here and there. That wicked, wicked gel had seduced her poor innocent boy. She turned as she heard the front door opening.

'Matthew!'

Enter Matthew Browne, still singing.

'Moonlight becomes you, it goes with your – Mother!'

From inside the bathroom came sounds of Lily re-emerging. Before Matt could push her back in she floated up to Mrs Browne.

'Lily!'

Matt hissed hopelessly and started to back out of the front door again. Too late. Lily had rushed towards him clad only in his dressing gown.

'Darling!'

'Matthew,' breathed his mother. 'What is going on? Who is this – this *person*?'

Matt tried to shake Lily off as if –

'This person? Who is this person? Who is this person? I don't know. Who are you person?'

'Who are you person? Really Matt – '

Lily winked heavily at Matt.

This should put a dampener on the acey-deucy bit.

'He's so absent-minded.'

She smiled sweetly at Queen Lesbia on the sofa.

'I'm his wife.'

When a man feels himself to be in the middle of a nightmare, he can do one of two things: he can run away and hope things will be better in the morning, or he can hide and hope things will be better in the morning. Not being someone to do anything in small measures Matt found himself doing both things, although not exactly in that sequence.

As soon as he could, he hid from his mother and Lily until such time as Lily was on her own, and then he re-emerged from under the table which had so often conveniently afforded him shelter from the more rampaging elements of his life, and flapped at Lily who was just coming in with a coffee tray.

'Have you got rid of her?'

'Of course I haven't got rid of her. She's gone to powder her beak. There was no need to go rushing off like that was there?'

'There was *every* need! What on earth inspired you to tell her you were my wife?'

'Safety precautions. To stop her getting at you.'

'Stop her getting at me? If she thinks I'm married she is going to get at me more than ever! I think I'd better explain – too late.'

He dived back under his table again, leaving Lily to stare at the place he had been and wonder what animal Matt so acutely resembled. Something that was there one minute and gone the next, a shy animal that lived in a hole and rarely came out. She had just decided that it was possibly an otter that was most like when the dreadful nympho made a dabbing and sniffing noise at her and sank down on the sofa, so forcing her to pay attention.

'I just do not believe all this is happening.'

'I know the feeling. Have some therapeutic coffee.'

Lily shoved a cup of coffee in front of her.

'This is all most upsetting.'

The disappointed sex maniac sniffed even more loudly, so loudly in fact that Lily had a good mind to tell her to blow her nose.

'Sit down. I want to talk to you. Where has Matthew gone?'

Really not content with scaring Matthew half to pieces this Operatic Insatiable wanted her at the same time too.

'Where has Matthew gone?' asked Lily. 'Oh, he just went out. You know. But he'll be back soon. So – how's the opera?'

A nice discussion about *La Traviata* might take her mind off other more inflammatory things.

'I am not here to talk about Opera,' breathed Madame fiercely.

Oh dear, what a pity, thought Lily, and then one second later realised that Madame's table, with her cup of coffee on it, was moving very quickly towards the door, which in the circumstances was hardly surprising since it had Matthew Browne underneath it.

'Where were we?' said Lily hopefully. 'Yes, the Opera.'

'Would you mind moving this table? I cannot reach my coffee.'

'No, no, it's much better to move the *sofa*. It's the floor you see. It's got this dreadful slope.'

Lily leapt behind the sofa and shoved Opera Star, sofa and all, towards the table.

'So?' she said, trying not to pant from her efforts. 'So you really believe Matt's a really talented nymphomaniac, I mean composer? I mean you really do?'

'Obviously. Otherwise why should I finance all this?'

'*You* finance all this?'

'I'm sure you're familiar with the old adage. Behind every man there's a woman – and in most cases it's his mother.'

'His mother? Oh you want to hear Matthew on the subject of his *mother*?' said Lily loudly, and wondered why the table, still complete with Matthew Browne Esquire, suddenly moved at an even greater speed towards the door.

'Perhaps,' said old Hatchet Face, 'you do not realise who I am, young lady?'

'Of *course* I realise who you are. Matt's told me all about you and your – lovely hats,' she ended helplessly.

'Then all I can say is that you are rapidly confirming my worst suspicions about the modern generation.'

With which observation the poor woman deposited her empty coffee cup where the table should have been, if it hadn't had Matt underneath it, and watched horrified while it crashed to the floor.

'Whoops – there goes that slope again. I'll get a bucket and stirrup pump,' cried Lily, and dashed out to the kitchen.

'I think I need a drink.'

Mrs Browne crossed to the drink table at the very same time as her son completed his escape from under the dressed table and shut the flat door behind him. This whole morning, a morning that had started out as a poem, had suddenly become sheer doggerel. What on earth was Lily doing? What had she been saying to his mother, or rather what *hadn't* she been saying to his mother? Air, air, he must get some air. He started to hurl himself down the stairs, the lift, entirely in keeping with the rest of the morning, having appeared to have stuck.

The lift in fact had stuck and what it had stuck *with* was Harold and Maria Bellcanto, *the* Maria Bellcanto – she of the hungry ways and warming habits. Why it had stuck with this twin burden was like many things quite simple, when you know the explanation.

The explanation was this. Maria Bellcanto, a person as entirely unknown to Harold the Porter as indeed she had proved to be to Lily Pond, passed Harold the Porter's loggia at just the moment he had finally lowered his copy of the *Sun*. Since it was the second posh hatted lady to pass his loggia that morning, and having learnt his manners from the first, Harold naturally put on his hat and leapt to his feet, in the approved manner.

'Mr Matthew Browne,' commanded the second hatted lady, leaving Harold to wonder if Mr Browne had suddenly changed his after-shave to one of those invincible mixtures that attracted ladies in the same way that aniseed is said to attract hounds.

'I have an appointment with him,' breathed the new paragon – 'Maria Bellcanto.'

'I'll tell him you're here,' said Harold obediently.

Miss Bellcanto appeared not to hear this, because she leant across his desk and made a little moue at him.

'Cheeky,' she said caressingly.

And then she held his hand firmly in his and breathed exotic perfume all over his uniform.

'Don't ring Mr Browne,' she said secretively, 'let's surprise him, shall we?'

'Up to you, Miss Bellcanter.'

Harold stared into Miss Bellcanto's eyes and felt himself being drawn against his will towards the lift. Still under her spell, he rang for it and then, when it arrived, stood back deferentially for her to get in. Her perfume was making him feel quite hot and dizzy, which must have been the reason why he found himself so completely unable to resist her insistence that he should 'drive the lift'.

He drove. And all he could say to himself afterwards was that it was one of the most bloomingest pieces of luck that Mr Browne lived on the fourth floor, and not the seventh, because what that Bellcanter woman managed to get up to between ground and fourth was more than his imagination had been able to evolve in a whole half hour's contemplation of Miss Angie Dunn's vital statistics on page three of the *Sun*. Blimey.

Meanwhile downstairs Matt was not unnaturally quite unable to find Harold, since he wasn't there. And then he suddenly remembered the house phone. If, as he had thought, on the way down those four flights of stairs, Lily had mistaken his mother for the well-known maniac Maria Bellcanto, then the obvious solution to all their problems was to ring and inform Lily of her colossal error, and then dart out for his bucket of badly needed fresh air.

'Hallo Matthew Browne's dugout – '

He could hear Lily's voice had assumed that cheerful hopeless tone that most people's voices usually assume when the roof has just fallen in and there is nothing more to do.

'Lily! It's Matt. I think you've got things a little confused – now listen carefully and do not rabbit. That woman is my *mother*. Understand? My mother.'

'Which woman? The one who's just arrived?'

Lily turned round and stared at Maria Bellcanto who – sorry, whom – she had just let into the flat.

'*Which* woman. Of course the woman who has just arrived.'

Matt sighed. Really Lily could be a little thick at times.

'The woman in the *hat*. She is my *mother*. So button that famous lip and don't come out with any more of your marriage fantasies. Okay? Say you're – say you're – just don't say anything. No – say you're the cleaner. And I'll be as quick as I can. I just must get some air!'

'Claustrophobia back again?'

'In spades.'

Matt slammed down Harold's house phone and ran towards the front door. Harold, emerging from his sensational lift ride saw him, but on account of the fact that his legs had become extremely incapacitated from his lift he could only call after Matthew weakly and be unsurprised that he didn't hear him.

Lily turned from the telephone and muttered 'the plot thickens' to herself, which was about the only way she could think of putting it, and went to join Matt's newly arrived mother in the main part of the drawing room.

'Well – ' she said brightly, 'that was Matt. He won't be long. Anyway – how do you do?'

She put out a hand that failed to find a counterpart to shake. Instead, there was a small silence while Mrs Browne, who was obviously some *siren*, pursed her lips and renewed her lipstick.

'I must say – ' Lily tried again. 'I must say you're even prettier than Matt said you were.'

'Of course I am!' agreed the exotic flower in front of her, 'of course I am. And who are you?'

She flared her nostrils at Lily.

'Oh – *me*. Me. You don't have to pay attention to me. I'm only the cleaner,' said Lily, remembering Matt's advice and quickly pulling a decrepit hankie out of his dressing gown pocket, and flapping it vaguely at some dust on the piano.

'The cleaner?'

'Yus. Yer don't want to pie no attention ter me.'

'Is Matthew not back yet?'

She of the operatic and other distinctions floated back into the room, still dabbing her face with a lace handkerchief.

'Is Matthew not back yet?' she asked again.

'Ah,' said exotic Mamma, 'you are here to see my Matthew as *well*?'

'Your Matthew?'

Lily breathed in deeply. She didn't know why but she didn't like the look of the situation, not at all did she. In fact if there was going to be a hat crash, she would rather not be there to witness the whole beastly business.

'I'm off,' she muttered.

'Stay where you are and introduce us,' one of them commanded.

'What?'

Lily re-assumed her cleaner's accent, an accent that she was only too well aware was *circa* 1894.

'Oh – yus. Of course you two don't know each other. Mrs Browne – Maria Bellcanter – Maria Bellcanter – Mrs Browne – Lily Pond – the bedroom.'

Upon which utterance she made good her escape and left the two hats to confront each other in whatever way they chose.

Mrs Browne stared after Lily.

'What an *extraordinary* creature.'

'Quite,' agreed Maria, 'not at all like the normal daily help.'

'Daily help? That girl is a daily help?'

'So she tells me.'

Mrs Browne collapsed upon the sofa.

'Matthew has married his daily help.'

'Matthew has married,' whispered Maria suddenly also stricken prone to the sofa. 'I don't believe it, it can't be true! Does he have no thought for *me*?'

'For *you*? Who are you?'

'And who *are* you?'

'I am his *mother*.'

'*I* am Maria Bellcanto.'

'Maria Bellcanto? Not Maria Bellcanto?'

'The Maria Bellcanto.'

Mrs Browne gasped.

'But I have *all* your recordings.'

'So – have *I*.'

'I am such an admirer of yours.'

Maria reached into her handbag and pulled out a photograph of Matthew as a young soloist.

'I too am an admirer of yours. To have produced such a wonderful son as my Matthew.'

Mrs Browne also reached into her handbag and brought out another photograph which she handed to Maria.

'This is Matthew at three with his first piano.'

'Ah,' Maria gazed soulfully at the photo, 'and has he really married that – *skivvy*?'

'He has really married that skivvy.'

'Ah – then I think I am going to swoon.'

She started to sink sideways.

'Good heavens, woman! Nobody swoons nowadays,' cried Mrs Browne.

'Except – for me. But then nostalgia is my forte,' whispered Maria, and suited the action to the words.

Mrs Browne sprang to her feet.

'Good heavens. Good Lord. What's your name! You in there!'

Lily re-appeared.

'You rang?'

'I shall need your help. The lady has fainted.'

Lily looked at the crumpled figure on the sofa.

'Oh dear was it something you said?'

'Don't be impertinent – and come and give me a hand.'

'Perhaps we ought to loosen her clothing and get her on the bed?'

'Oh yes – loosen my clothing and get me on the *bed*,' murmured the recumbent figure.

Lily seized hold of it and between them they managed to get her on to Matt's bed.

Mrs Browne looked at the immobile Opera Star and wondered if she needed sal volatile, or smelling salts?

'There's nothing like eating hay when you're faint,' quoted Lily.

'Don't be absurd. Smelling salts are much better.'

'I didn't say there was nothing *better* said the King. I said there was nothing *like* it.'

Mrs Browne stared at Lily and shook her head.

'I can't think what inspired him to do it.'

She swept out with Lily trailing behind.

'Economy,' said Lily informatively, 'he realised if he married me he wouldn't have to pay my insurance stamp.'

'Psshaw.'

'Pssaw?'

'Psst,' came from behind Lily making her jump.

'Don't *do* that, Matt.'

'How's it all going?'

'Terrific. Your singing friend's preparing a poultice for your mother who's passed out in her bedroom.'

'My *mother* passed out? I don't believe it.'

'You'd better go and see her.'

Matt hesitated. Now he was back beside Lily he was loath not unnaturally to abandon her for his mother, to name but a thousand.

'Go on.'

He went, just as the fearful Opera lady returned.

'I thought I heard Matthew.'

'You did. He's just administering to the sick.'

'In that case, perhaps while he's out of the way we could have a little talk. There are one or two facts I think you ought to know.'

'It's all right. My mother gave me one of those booklets when I was twelve.'

Mrs Browne ignored this.

'I may appear to be old-fashioned to you,' she continued inexorably, 'but I know about girls like you. Out for what you can get. What you probably don't realise is that if – if Matt married without the Trust's approval, then he would lose *all* this.'

This was too much for Lily.

'I must say, for an itinerant troubadour, you're very genned up on the private life of Mr Matthew Browne.'

Bristle, bristle, she'd finally had quite enough of Madame La Opera Star.

'*Itinerant troubadour*. I am his *mother*.'

'And I'm to be Queen of the May. That woman in there is his mother.'

Suddenly, quite suddenly, Lily had that feeling that she was not only wearing two left shoes, but that she had stepped in a whatsit right up to her thingummy. Môche, it couldn't be, could it? No, surely not?

'No? That woman in there is not his mother?'

'No.'

'The woman in *here* is his mother. Matt? There's a woman in here who says she's your mother!'

Lily went to knock on an already opening door. Matt re-appeared looking much as if he had just been dragged through a hedge backwards, and then forwards again.

'Of course she's my mother,' he gasped.

'And the woman in there – '

'The woman in there is – is just a little over-excited.'

'What have you been doing to that woman in there?'

Matt turned to his mother.

'I haven't been doing anything to that woman in there. It's what that woman in there has been trying to do to *me*.'

'Maria Bellcanto?'

'Yes, Maria Bellcanto,' shouted Matt above the noise of the madwoman banging on the bedroom door.

'No woman who can soar to such heights with "Granada" would want to sink to such depths with *you*. I knew you were up to something when you sent me flowers on my birthday. I suspected it might be a girl, but not a skivvy. And to go and get *married* to her. This is not the sort of girl you were brought up to marry. You may – associate with girls like this, but you do not marry them. And is she really worth all this sacrifice?'

Mrs Browne gestured round the flat and, to tell the truth as Lily's eye followed her hand, she could see exactly what she meant. It *was* a really lovely flat and Matt was the sort of person who needed and *deserved* a really lovely flat.

Matt however didn't seem to be much taken with this point, because he merely frowned slightly and asked his mother, 'Would you really carry out that threat?'

'I certainly would. This is not the sort of girl I had in mind for you.'

Lily wondered, just for a second, if there was anything she could possibly do at this late stage to bring Mrs Browne into line with being able to think that Lily Pond from Streatham was more suitable than perhaps she realised. But then it would take an optimist of an even more incurable nature than Miss Pond to think that a woman who had been hurled about her own flat, mistaken for a lesbian and a nymphomaniac, and finally called an itinerant troubadour – well, it would take someone more *imaginative* than Mrs Browne to be able to see *through* all the morning's goings-on to the true gold that was Lily. Ha, ha.

'You don't have to worry, Mother, we're not married, and

I can faithfully promise you that after today Lily is never coming back to this flat again.'

He turned to Lily grim faced.

'Now pick up your bag and say good-bye nicely.'

'Good-bye nicely. Why?'

'Because you're going home.'

'Because I'm going home.'

'Go on.'

Lily went.

Matt turned to his mother.

'One day all this will be *yours* and today's the day. Catch.'

He threw his keys at his mother, as hard as was impolite but not dangerous, and shut the flat door behind him.

'So.'

Lily pressed the lift bell.

'She's right you know. It would be silly to sacrifice all that.'

'I'm not sacrificing anything. The word sacrifice implies a loss. I may be losing a flat but I'm gaining a Lily.'

There was a pause as they both waited for the lift to arrive.

'I only own a grand piano, Lily.'

'So?'

'Have you thought what it's going to be like starting off married life with just a grand piano?'

'Hang about.'

Lily put her hands on her hips.

'What's all this rabbit about marriage? I don't remember marriage ever being mentioned ever before.'

'What are you talking about?'

'You haven't actually asked me actually to marry you.'

'Asked you? What's the point in asking you? You're going to, aren't you?'

'Of course I'm going to,' said Lily crossly.

'So what's the point in asking you?'

Matt opened the lift door.

'Going my way?'

CHAPTER SEVEN

It Nearly Happened One Night

It was all very well for Matt to assume that she was going to marry him (which of course she was), Lily thought as she stood as still as she could in a brown paper cut-out of a wedding dress, but it did give rise to several buts.

'Please stand still, Lily,' sighed her mother, through a mouthful of pins.

'I am standing still, Ma,' Lily replied.

'Then stand even stiller.'

In fact, pondered Lily returning to her ruminations, it gave rise to several seemingly unanswerable buts. Like 'but how could they afford it'. And 'but where's the money going to come from' – now that Matt's dreadful mother had cut him off without a penny and what with Lily's family being more than a mite penniless themselves, which was why Lily was standing as still as she could in the family living room in a brown paper cut-out of a facsimile of Princess Anne's wedding dress, which her mother was trying her best to translate into sumptuous reality, while the bridegroom-to-be paced nervously around the perimeter of the room periodically and anxiously examing the impoverished contents of a rather sinister looking purse.

Her mother tugged some creases out of the paper cut-out and sighed again.

'A wedding in the family,' she said shaking her head. 'If only your father was alive to see it.'

'Bet he never thought I'd be getting married as a parcel,' quizzed Lily in a feeble attempt to bring some jollity to the proceedings. But Matt was not to be thus lightened.

'Look,' he suddenly interrupted. 'Can we just get this absolutely straight?'

It was Lily's turn to sigh – which she did extravagantly – because she knew which direction the conversation was once more going to take. They were back to the buts.

'But there is nothing *to* get straightened, Matt,' said her mother firmly from the floor. 'You don't pay for nothing.'

'I've got to pay for something,' Matt replied. 'It says so in this little book.'

He waved the Moss Bros Guide to wedding etiquette.

'But you haven't any bunce!' Lily once more protested. 'So how can you pay for something?'

Lily's little grandmother pulled her Russian shawl tightly around her shoulders and snorted at the silent but still flickering television screen.

'Stuff,' she said. 'That's all you people nowadays think about. Money, money, money. You should do just what you feel like doing and let the devil take the hindposts.'

'That,' replied Matt, 'is this sort of philosophy that brought about the fall of Rome.'

'Then if that is the case,' snorted Littlema, 'you must avoid the Holy City on your travels.'

Lily's mother stood up and surveyed her handiwork.

'Mmm,' she said, slapping her daughter lightly on her brown papered derrière, 'off you go and change. We'll finish it in front of Perry Mason.'

'Okeydoke,' agreed Lily, only too pleased to be granted her release from the living room. People talking about money always made her hot, so with unbounded relief she crackled out of the room.

Matt, however, was not so anxious to let sleeping dogs lie, so he sat himself down on the sofa next to Littlema, and once more peered inside his purse, in the vain hope that his few remaining pound notes might mysteriously have multiplied.

'I've got a few pounds,' he muttered. 'I've got about twenty-five pounds in fact. I could take her *somewhere* on a honeymoon.'

Mrs Pond packed up her patterns and smiled.

'You have your honeymoon when you're in ship plasters again. There'll be time enough.'

Matt had long ago given up any attempt to understand Mrs Pond's verbiage, as at this very moment he was more than sure that she was right, that they would have to postpone the honeymoon, until such time as they were in 'ship plasters' again. There seemed very little point in continuing any more discussion about the aforesaid honeymoon.

'Stuff. Stupid man. Maybe I get rich next week.'

Littlema turned off the television, and threw her football coupon in the wastepaper basket. Then she turned, and to Matt's surprise came and sat down next to him. For the first time she took one of her future grandson-in-law's hands in hers.

'So?' she asked sweetly, 'where you go for your honeymoon?'

Mrs Pond waved the Princess Anne brown paper replica at Littlema.

'*Mother.*'

But as everyone who has ever owned a granny knows – there is no stopping them.

'Oh Lily loved the thought of the honeymoon. Ever since she was a small child in plaits.'

'Let's have some tea,' said Mrs Pond forcibly.

'Yes,' continued Littlema, 'she always had this dream since, since I took her for tea on her tenth birthday to the Claremont. "Littlema," she say, with a face full of wonder and the orchestra playing *Oklahoma*, "Littlema, when I get marr-ied I spend the wedding night in this wonderful shebang." She was in love with it. She always talk of it ever since.'

Matt looked into Littlema's shrewd grey eyes.

'The Claremont? I'm not sure we could quite stretch to the Claremont.'

He hesitated. Littlema lent forward and gave him a lavender embrace, or what Lily would call a 'granny special'. All of a sudden Matt found himself wondering why one night, just one night at the Claremont wouldn't, after all, be within their reach.

Matt's entry into the Claremont twenty-four hours later was somewhat slowed by his now conditioned reaction to his newly won poverty, namely preoccupation with the contents of his purse. Just as he had checked his remaining funds for the fourteenth time, he found himself with the feeling that he was being watched, which indeed he was. The gentleman behind the desk was looking at him, and looking at him in such a way as to suggest that he better have business of some nature in the Claremont, or he, the gentleman behind the desk, would have no hesitation in showing him el door.

Matt crept up to the desk, wondering why it was that the knowledge that you had no money made such a difference to your confidence. A few weeks ago he would have felt perfectly at ease at the Claremont. It was somewhere where he had frequently met his mother for lunch, or some dear old ageing great aunt, or some very un-dear equally ageing record producer, and he would have had no problem in *going* up to the desk, and stating his purpose, instead of *sidling* up as he was now, and clearing his throat several times, before asking for someone to show him a room that might be suitable for a – for a – well, suitable, for a er, a er.

The assistant coughed discreetly to distract Matt's attention from his purse.

'This is the least – large of our rooms, sir. Though still – I think you would find – very comfortable.'

'And this is?'

'This is?'

It was Matt's turn to give a discreet cough, accompanied by a very indiscreet mime of 'money'.

'Oh – '

The assistant picked up the mime, and repeated it himself.

'The room itself with breakfast for two – is fourteen guineas.'

'Fourteen guineas? That's fourteen pounds – '

'Fourteen shillings, sir.'

'Fourteen shillings, sir.'

Matt had another quick look in his purse.

'You couldn't do it for – no, no, that's fine. We'll take it. Fine.'

And then he added extremely sotto voce 'I think'.

There is very little anyone can add to the eloquent descriptions that have been heaped upon that sublime state known as love. As Lily trotted in front of the bellboy towards their room at the Claremont, she had indeed the very same sumptuous feeling of unreality that she had so often read accompanied the Great Emotion. Nothing Matt could have done for her, no way of demonstrating his love could have been so supremely effective as this incredible gesture of booking them into the Claremont on their honeymoon night. And this was all before she saw the room in – no, into which, they had been booked.

'Oh Ikey – will you just look?'

Matt was too busy trying to calculate the proper percentage for the bellboy's tip to turn around.

'Come on, Lily,' he muttered, 'it's not exactly the bridal suite.'

Honestly, typical.

'Well, what do you think it is?'

Lily's hand gestured towards the room, and as she did so Matt's eyes took in one of the most splendid rooms he'd seen since he once had to meet Rory Vox with a view to his, Rory Vox, buying some of Matt's songs.

'It's the bridal suite?'

Matt's head spun.

'The bridal suite at the Claremont.'

Lily took Matt's hands in hers. Talk about 'My Hero'.

'The bridal suit at the Claremont,' she said again, to make sure she was hearing herself right. 'I know you said you had a surprise for me, but this is ridiculous.'

'Hear, hear,' said Matt. 'This isn't our room. This is *not* our room, Lily.'

But Lily hadn't heard him. She was too busy running in and out of the rooms.

'Oh Matt! Matt! Wait till you see! Wait till you see the bedroom.'

'There's a bedroom as well?'

'Matt – how did you *know*?'

Matt, far from being remotely tempted to clasp Lily in his arms, and tell her it was all due to Granny, was rushing about the room inspecting the names on the flowers. After all, the names on the flowers were sure to reveal the rightful owner of this suite.

'To dearest – Matt – and – Lily – all – love – Ma – and – Littlema.'

'But this is not the room I *booked*.'

Lily re-emerged from the other room.

'Oh Matt. I shan't forget this. Not ever. Not as long as I ever shall live never.'

Matt looked at Lily hesitatingly.

'Look – Lily.'

Lily held up a restraining hand.

'And you're not to tell me what it cost either.'

'I'll try not to – but Lily – '

'Now I must ring my mother. Wait till she hears!'

'You must? Right? Right.'

As usual at most crisis points of his life, Matt felt an overriding desire for air, any air, but not the air belonging to the Bridal Suite, which probably cost an extra ten guineas a night anyway. He started to back towards the door.

'I think I'll just er – '

'Could I have 224–1143, please?'

Lily turned round, but Matt was gone. Fled. Vamoosed. She smiled at where he had been. Silly old Ratface, anyone would think from the surprise on his face that he hadn't seen the Bridal Suite before.

The foyer was very busy, and the desk very crowded. Matt made one or two feeble attempts to attract the notice of the man behind the desk, and then gave up dejectedly. It was useless, quite useless. He went behind a convenient pillar and tried to think. The best thing to do would be to telephone someone. In an emergency there was nothing quite like telephoning someone, but who? It was too late to phone the bank for a loan, and since he was now married far too late to phone his mother for one either, and completely inappropriate to phone Lily's mother for anything at all. The situation was a nightmare. The contents of his purse would hardly cover early morning tea in the bridal suite, let alone a ham sandwich with watercress on top. He must do something. And, as they say in the best fiction – quickly. He fled to the telephone booth.

'584–6101?'

Through the glass booth he could see the desk clerk answering his call.

'The Claremont, London. Can I help you?'

'Yes, yes – yes, I rikwiresome informazzion please.'

For some reason, best not known, he found himself assuming an Indian accent.

'I'm sorry, Madam? Some information?'

Madam? He had no idea his voice had gone that squeaky.

'Yes, yes, oh my goodness yes, and it's "sir". I am rekwiring to know how much for your bridal suite when I can come and had the bed and breakfast there?'

'The bridal suite is sixty guineas a night sir. Hello, sir? Are you still there? Sir?'

'Oh my goodness – sixty guineas? Oh my goodness me. Thank you I will be letting you know. Sixty guineas. Oh my goodness gracious me.'

He put the telephone down, and wandered back into the foyer again. Oh my goodness, oh my goodness, how on earth would he tell Lily? He muttered 'oh my goodness' for the tenth time and then found himself wandering by mistake into the bar, and then since he was, after all, there, wandering up to the counter in search of the one thing he needed most at this moment – a drink.

'Brandy, please,' he muttered to the barman.

The two old gentlemen who were presently occupying the bar stools beside him looked at him curiously. One of them tapped him on the arm.

'He who aspires to be a hero must drink brandy, eh? Just seen the hotel ghost?'

'In a manner of speaking.'

The younger of the two nodded knowledgeably.

'Looks damn wobbly. Have a draft.'

Matt stared into the meagre contents of his wallet, and shook his head. He couldn't start getting involved in buying rounds, when it was going to take all he had to get in and out of this place without being arrested.

'No, no, look – it's very kind of you but – the way things are – '

'Bit short on the old pelf, eh? All right then spoof me for it.'

'Sorry?'

'Spoof you know spoofing surely?'

'No.'

'Good heavens, Bert, chap doesn't know spoofing.'

'Good heavens, Tommy, would you credit it?'

Bert shook his head at Matt, and then proceeded to demonstrate the art of spoofing to him. He laid a clean pound note upon the bar counter, and covered it with his hand.

'Go on then, young fellah,' said Tommy encouragingly, 'call the Queen.'

'The Queen?'

Bert nodded.

'Betty up or Betty down.'

'Oh right – Betty up or – '

Bert quickly uncovered his pound and looked at which way the pound was facing.

'Betty up! Damn me, Tommy. Damn my eye. He's won. Double or quits?'

'Double or quits?'

'Up or down?'

'Sorry? Oh – Betty up.'

Bert again uncovered the note.

'Betty up. Damn, damn, he's done me again.'

He pushed the money towards Matt.

'Drinks on me, George.'

'This is mine?'

'Of course it is,' said Tommy, 'yer won the spoof.'

Matt looked at his newly won fortune of two pounds.

'Quite a game this.'

Bert waggled his moustache reprovingly.

'It's not a game young fellah, it's a callin',' he said reverently.

'Well batted. Damn good.'

Tommy raised his glass.

Matt attempted to look modest.

'Beginner's luck, I'm afraid.'

'Damn good.'

Tommy chucked his tot down in one.

'Same again?'

Matt shook his head.

'No – no I really mustn't, no I really must go. But I can't tell you – ' he waved his hand vaguely to take in the bar, 'it's been wonderful. It's a very good game. Perhaps you'll be around later?'

'Course old chap. Always around for a bit of a game.'

'I might see you?'

Tommy nodded.

'Always around for a bit of a game.'

Matt hesitated for a moment, tempted by the idea of staying and perhaps doubling his winnings, but Tommy and Bert were already on to pastures new, new fields of recreation.

'George, a pound you can't pour two large ones without the measure.'

'Damn good. Pound says you can't, damn good.'

And on.

Lily looked at her watch. There was no doubt about it Matt had been gone longer than was surely proper in a bridegroom on his honeymoon night. She had now straightened her dress, powdered her nose, and sprayed herself with 'Intimate' so many times, that if he proved to be much longer she would be so over-powdered, and smelling so strong, that he would be completely put off. But, hush, was not that his quick light step in the corridor without? She opened the door.

'Hello stranger.'

Matt nodded absently at her. Lily handed him a glass of champagne.

'Hope you don't mind – I've rung for dinner.'

Matt looked at her no longer in the least bit vague, but suddenly all too much present.

'You've rung for dinner. What did you go and ring for dinner for?'

Good heavens he was making dinner sound like something only practised by madmen.

'Parce que – j'ai faim. Rattle rattle.'

'We can't have dinner here!'

'Have you got a better wheeze? I can't think of any place nicer.'

'Of course there are places nicer. We could – we could go to your mother's!'

'My mother's?'

'At least it's free!'

Then hastily correcting himself.

'And easy. Nice and free and easy. This place is a bit – '

'Yes?'

'It's a bit – hot.'

Lily's eyes widened.

'Oh. Don't you like this place? I think this place is wonderful.'

'Of course it's wonderful! Marvellous. Even more than I thought it would be. Yes – it's certainly a lot more than I thought it would be.'

'You'll be better for some dinner.'

There was a discreet knock at the door.

'Entrez,' called Lily.

Matt turned round, and this time it was his eyes that widened. Not one trolley but two made their entrance, silently, discreetly, and extremely expensively. Silver domed covers sheltered avocados filled with prawns, roast ducklings lying smugly in their orange sauce, and a bombe surprise packed around with little chips of ice that sparkled like diamonds, and as far as Matt was concerned might as well *be* diamonds, for all that he could afford it.

'A cheese omelette would have been fine,' he muttered weakly.

Lily laughed.

'Honestly, Ratface, a cheese omelette – on your wedding night?'

Matt tugged at his collar again.

'It would have been fine,' he said.

In fact he managed to eat his way through the three courses without much of a hitch, but no one could say the conversation exactly flowed. Possibly a bridegroom who is busy trying to add up in his head the maximum charge possible for avocado pears with prawns, and roast duck with new potatoes, isn't the best companion, but to Lily, Matt was wonderful if a little nervous, which was understandable, after all *she* was a little nervous, and she didn't suffer from having an artistic temperament the way Matt did.

'You're still not very relaxed, are you? I know. Let's play a game. Games are good for relaxing people. Handsome cash prizes. For a thousand pretend pounds, what colour are my eyes?'

'Blue.'

'Wrong – grey. Two things people invariably get wrong. The colour of their partner's eyes and the names of the Seven Dwarfs.'

'Everybody knows the names of the Seven Dwarfs.'

Lily did a little drum roll on the edge of the table.

'Right then for two thousand pounds, the names of the Seven Dwarfs.'

'Grumpy. Grumpy – Bashful – *Doc*. Doc – Grumpy – Bashful – Sleepy – Dozy?'

'No Dozy.'

Matt frowned.

'Sleepy – Bashful – Doc – Grumpy – '

He tried again.

Sleepy – Bashful – Grumpy – Doc –'

Lily took over.

'Sleepy – Bashful – Doc – Grumpy – Sneezy – Dopey and Happy.'

'Of course! Sneezy, Dopey and Happy. And nobody ever remembers them?'

Lily shook her head.

'Nobody.'

'Really?'

Matt put down his heavy white linen napkin.

'Where are you going?'

'Won't be long,' he said curtly, because he had suddenly been seized by the idea that he might have a present solution to his future problem, i.e., the bill. He started to walk towards the door then remembering his bride of four hours he turned, 'Look – you run the bath. I'm just going to go and stretch my legs. I always like to stretch my legs before I turn in.'

'Why? Aren't they long enough?'

Lily got up.

'I'll come with you.'

'No, no,' said Matt hurriedly. 'No I mean you can't. It's traditional. On this sort of – for a man to – around the block while the – slips into – something. I won't be long.'

He pulled at the nearest door handle.

'Except that's a cupboard. Won't be a minute.'

Lily stared after him.

'Grumpy, Dopey or just Bashful?'

Meanwhile her errant bridegroom made his way swiftly to the downstairs bar. He only hoped that the two old fellows would be there, and more important, still game for a spoof. As he rounded the corner, he knew instantly that he need never have doubted them. Bert and Tommy were still there, and although more than a few doubles must have passed swiftly down their well-bred throats since Matt had seen them at half past six, their positions at the bar remained strictly unaltered.

'Ah hello again.'

Matt found himself rubbing his hands together.

Bert nudged Tommy.

'Fellah's back.'

'Fellah's come back to play? What shall we play? Eh?'

'How about some more spoofing?'

'Finished spoofing' old chap. That's just a pipeopener. We're on to the big stuff now.'

Bert cleared his throat, and passed a challenging hand around his moustache.

'The big stuff?' asked Matt warily.

'Breathholding. Guess the cherries in the jar. Chucking nuts into ladies handbags, tip toeing and throwing the cat.'

'Throwing the cat! What on earth is throwing the cat?'

Tommy glanced up at George the barman.

'Not allowed to play it anymore,' he said sulkily, 'George doesn't approve.'

'So what do you want to lose your dibs at, eh? Guess the cherries? Breathholding?'

Bert looked hopefully at Matt. He loved breathholding.

'I was rather hoping for a few spoofs.'

'Very well. We can always oblige an old customer while he makes up his mind.'

'Same as before?'

'Damn decent,' said Tommy mistaking the order, 'large brand – '

'George,' called Bert, 'three large brands.'

He pulled yet another newly ironed pound note from his wallet.

'Up or down?'

'Please let it be up – Betty up.'

They both looked down.

'Tought T old fruit, she's not lookin' at yer.'

Bert shook his head sympathetically. Matt tipped his back, and swiftly poured the brandy down his throat. Courage, courage, faint heart never won fair lady.

'Drouble or quits, bubble or dits, double or quits?'

'Can't lose. Can't lose,' Bert agreed.

'Up or down?'

'Betty up!'

'Betty up!'

'God Save The Queen!'

'That's mine.'

Bert took Matt's money.

'And three pounds for the round, sir,' George whispered.

'And three pounds for the round.'

Matt handed George the money.

'Back to square one.'
'Let old Tom have a go.'
'Yes,' said Tommy, 'let old me have a go.'
'Up or down old fruit?'
Tommy frowned.
'Betty up,' he said at last.
They all looked down.
'Betty up.'
'Damn good, Tommy. Well played, sir. Another one to Tommy.'
Matt passed Tommy yet another one of his fast dwindling pound notes.
'Always up on the oncers. Don't know why, always up on the oncers.'
Bert leant across the bar.
'Just one round of throwin' the cat, George. Young fellah here's never seen it done.'
George shook his head firmly.
'I'm afraid not, Your Grace. I believe some of the bus passengers are still in hospital.'
'Damn shame.'
Bert's face fell, and then brightened again.
'How about a fiver on round the room without touching the floor?'
'Sorry Your Grace,' George interrupted, 'sedentary games only.'
Matt gazed forlornly into his purse. Something had to be done and soon, but meanwhile it was time for another round, and another game. Guess the cherries in the jar? Breath-holding? Breathholding it was. Bert sucked in his breath, and started to turn purple. One, two, three, four, five, six, seven...
Later, much later, when all that was left of his honeymoon fund was a single five pound note, Matt turned in desperation to Lily – poor Lily's game. It had to be explained slowly and carefully because none of them were the same as when they had first started, whenever it was.
'It's easy. I juss arse – ask you questions, and you juss answer my questions.'
'For handsome cash prizes?'
'For handsome cash prizes. General knowledge only. No trick questions. Right.'
He did Lily's drum roll on the bar.

'Right.'
'Right.'

Both old gentlemen looked at him, ready for anything. Matt slapped a five pound note, his last five pound note on the table.

For five pounds – what are the eyes of your wife's colour? The colour of your wife's eyes?'

'Blue.'

Matt shook his head.

'Blue.'

'Wrong,' said Matt promptly.

'Wrong?'

'Nobody ever gets the colour of your wife's eyes right! Wrong.'

'They're blue,' said Bert indignantly. 'Good Gawd she's known around the Hunt as old Bunty Blue Eyes. They're blue all right.'

He took Matt's last five pound note. Now he was into credit.

'Next question?' demanded Tommy.

'Next question,' said Matt desperately, 'next question, to be – for ten pounds.'

Bert raised his eyebrows.

'For ten pounds?'

'The names of the Seven Dwarfs.'

'Easy.'

Matt raised a hand.

'One at a time, and you have one minute from – *now*.'

Another drum roll on the bar.

'Damn good.'

Bert took a deep breath.

'Grumbly. That's one of the buggers. Grumbly – Doc – Dozy.'

'No Dozy.'

'No Dozy eh? Grumbly – Doc ah – *Sleazy*.'

'No Sleazy!'

'Grumbly, Doc – Sleazy, Snoopy – Grumbly, Doc Sleazy, Sloopy – '

'Five seconds!'

'Grumbly Doc Sleazy Sloopy Beaky Mitch and Titch.'

He sat back defeated.

'Wrong,' said Matt trying to keep the relief out of his voice.

'Dammit.'

Bert handed him over ten pounds, and Matt saw the road to riches once more stretching before him.

'Well played, sir. What are the little buggers' names?'

Tommy interrupted.

'No, don't tell us! It's my go! Grumpy, Bashful, Doc. Grumpy Bashful, Doc, – Sneezy.'

'No Sneezy!'

'Sleepy! How many have I got?'

'Five! And ten seconds to go!'

'Sleepy, GRUMPY BASHFUL, DOC, SNEEZY, SLEEPY, SLEEPY SNOOZY AND – HUMPY!'

Bert shook his head reprovingly.

'No Humpy. Remember what your doctor said.'

'Your time is up,' said Matt, with a desire to kiss the next two fivers that came across the bar towards him.

'I want another go! We'll get him this time, Bert!'

'Right. I'm game! Bashful – '

'One – '

'Grumpy!'

'Two!'

'Doc!'

'Three!'

And so on they went, while George smiled benignly, and set up yet another round of Napoleon's favourite beverage.

Upstairs however, in the bridal suite, all was not one long round of merriment. In fact the feelings of a bride who has not seen her groom for more than three hours after their honeymoon dinner might be said to be unprintable. Lily had a pretty good imagination, and although she might have imagined many things that *could* have happened to her and Matt between the church and the bridal suite – the complete disappearance of the aforesaid Matt was *not* one of them. It was true her thoughts had wandered in the hours after she had bathed and changed into her negligee and matching nightie and brushed her flowing blonde tresses – they had wandered from murder to assassination, and back again. The 'wait till I get hold of him' line of thought was not particularly original perhaps, but it was at least satisfying in a masochistic kind of way. As was hurling copies of *Vogue* and *Harpers Bazaar* at the chimney-piece while shouting 'marbles'.

'Marbles!'

Down in the bar, Matt and his drinking companions were not alone. Matt, the unbeaten holder of the answer to question number two, 'what are the names of the Seven Dwarfs', had now collected a crowd around him, each one more eager than the other to rob him of his now extremely swollen funds.

'Ten secinze.'

He stood in a corner of the room while yet another lady in a cocktail hat tried her luck.

'Grumpy Snoozy.'

'No Snoozy!'

'Grumpy Bashful Sloozy Sleepy Doc and *Droopy*!'

'Wrong!'

The woman returned to the throng.

'Charles you oaf, you swore there was a Droopy.'

'My go, my go,' said an old gentleman who had been queuing to try his luck.

Matt shook his head.

'I thin I god enuff now.'

He turned to Bert.

'Here. I wrode the names down here. Get your money back from the seethin mazzes.'

Bert took the piece of paper.

'Damn decent, damn decent,' he said touched.

Tommy put an arm round Matt.

'And if you hear of anywhere where we can throw a cat – just give us a tootle.'

'Damn good show.'

They all smiled at each other. Comrades, brothers in arms, heroes all.

The last Matt saw of them the crowd had surrounded them, and Bert, his moustache fluffed out with joy, was preparing to take on allcomers.

'Damn good show,' Matt muttered happily, and made his way towards the Bridal Suite.

'Liddy! Liddy! Liddy id's all right now, Liddy! Everythin's all right now. You can have your dream come true.'

He kept calling all the way up the stairs. Stairs, and stairs, and more stairs, and then at last Liddy all beautiful standing in the door in a wonderful white thing.

'Matt?'

Matt leant across the threshold, and fell into the room.

'I love you, Liddy.'

'Matt where have you been? It's quarter past twelve, Matt.'

'I know, but it's all ride now Liddy. We doan have to worry bout a thin.'

He threw some of the money into the air.

'We doan have to worry about a thin.'

He sunk into the nearest chair, and quite suddenly oblivion overcame him.

'Matt? *Matt?*'

'Sleepy, Doc, Happy but Sleepy.'

Matt slept.

Lily looked down at him.

'Oh Matt.'

The following morning found them anxiously waiting by the desk in the foyer.

'Are you quite sure you've got enough now, Matt?'

'Of course I've got enough now,' croaked Matt.

Lily smiled at him, and slipped her arm through his. Trust Ratface to get himself in such a fantastic drama on his wedding night.

'There we are, Mr Browne – your bill.'

The Manager smiled at them.

'Thank you.'

Matt started to count the money out on to the desk.

'Ten, twenty, thirty, forty – fifty.'

'Excuse me, sir – '

The Manager leant forward discreetly.

Matt shook his head.

'It's all right I've got plenty, don't worry. Sixty seventy – '

'No, no, the point is that *is* plenty, sir, the bill is only twenty-five pounds sixteen shillings, sir.'

'Twenty-five pounds sixteen shillings. How can it be twenty-five pounds sixteen shillings? We had the *Bridal Suite*!'

'Of course you did, sir.'

The Manager smiled again.
'It's the custom of this hotel, if the bridal suite is free, to lend it to any newly wedded couple we might have staying.'
'*Lend* it. *Lend* it? You mean for the – same – '
'Of course, sir. Exactly. I'll get you some change.'
He started to walk away, but Matt stopped him.
'No – excuse me?'
'Sir?'
'Is the Bridal Suite still free?'
'I believe it is, sir.'
Matt took a firmer grip on Lily's hand.
'I think we'd like to stay a little longer.'
'Very good, sir. It will be our pleasure.'
He hit the bell.
'Boy?'
Matt looked at Lily.
'Well – I think that was the nightmare. Now let's have the dream.'

CHAPTER EIGHT

Three is None

One of the most disappointing aspects of life is the way things keep turning out just the way everyone else predicted they would. For instance Lily had been told, by more than one sage, that she would quarrel more in the first year of her marriage than at any other time. Although this was a prediction that she had been more than anxious to prove wrong, she was not quite sure that she had actually yet succeeded. Quite frankly, there were times when Matt proved so unbearably irritating that, had she been a very physical sort of person, she could quite easily have boxed his ears. As it was, ear boxing not being in her line, she was reduced to making her presence felt in other ways, not all of them totally effective. For instance – sniffing. Sniffing could be a good weapon, if Matt was not practising his piano, or demanding total hush so he could compose.

And sighing, sighing could also be good. Tonight she was trying sighing, because Matt was so sleepy he probably couldn't hear something as small as a sniff, whereas a good gutsy sigh, right from the pit of the tum, could get the whole bed moving, and with it – Matt.

'Lily?'

Lily did not deign to reply.

'You all right, Lily?'

Matt's anxious voice came out of the dark and if Lily hadn't been in such a bad mood with him, she would probably have just felt reassured that he still minded if she *was* all right or not, and then gone to sleep, but as it was such was her sense of grievance, not even his evident concern for her would stop her giving another, deep, deep sigh.

'Are you all right?' Matt asked again.

There was a pause and then Lily spoke.

'Of course I'm all right,' she said in her most un-all right voice.

'Then go to sleep then.'

Matt re-settled himself. Lily lay there for a minute thinking some very un-all right thoughts. Such as 'Has the Romance Gone Out of My Marriage?' and 'Is the Honeymoon Finally Over?' Gone were the first delirious days of marriage when Matt came home burdened with strawberries and loaded with champagne – leaving them to live off air for the rest of the week. Gone were the whole week-ends when feet only touched the carpet for the essentials of life, only to return a few minutes later for The Essential. Gone, gone. Gone, gone. Now all was seriousness. Matt working all day. She at home waiting for him to come back. Everything had stopped so quickly. She bit her lip and gave another shuddering sigh.

'Why shouldn't I be all right?' she demanded suddenly.

'Sssh, go to sleep.'

Matt continued to try to do so himself.

There was a silence. Then into the darkness:

'I can't.'

'Can't what?'

'Can't go to sleep.'

'Why not?'

Lily turned over – hard.

'Nothing. You wouldn't understand.'

'What wouldn't I understand?'

'Nothing.'

Matt sat up and put his light on.

'And how can I get to sleep if you keep putting on your light?'

'There's something bothering you.'

He'd noticed.

'How do you know there's something bothering me?'

'By the turmoil under the duvet.'

'I am perfectly all right.'

'You are? And nothing's bothering you?'

'Niet.'

'Fine.'

Matt settled down again and turned the light off.

Lily stared at the ceiling. Honestly, absolutely typical of a man to take your word for it. Who else but a man would take your word for it that you were fine, just because you *said* you were fine, when it was quite obvious that just because you said you were fine, didn't at all mean that you were. Men were so *straightforward*.

'Everything's fine except the fact that I haven't got any friends. Did you hear what I said, Matt?'

'Yes,' said Matt flatly, 'I heard what you said, Lily.'

'And?'

'Go to sleep.'

Lily stared hatefully at his unmoving all-male back.

'Go to sleep yourself.'

'I'm trying.'

Another silence and then, 'It's all right for you men.'

'What is all right for us men?'

'Nothing. It's just that you really have it all sewn up.'

'We've had all this out before, Lily.'

Matt put his light on again.

'I thought you were meant to be going to sleep?'

'About your friends and mine. We've had all this out.'

'It's no problem for you. You don't *have* any friends.'

'Of course I have friends!'

'Who?'

'You. I have you.'

'*And?*'

'I don't need any friends besides you. You're all the friends I need.'

He looked at her victorious.

'Below the belt,' she muttered crossly.

'Now can we get some sleep?'

Mr Browne switched off his light and settled down once more. Lily too turned off her light, but not for long. If he thought he could get away with it as lightly as that, he would have another thought coming.

'Well I do.'

'You do *what*?'

This was accompanied by an anguished sigh. She was getting through. On came the light.

'Need friends, Matt. I need friends. Specially now you're out all day recording and you've stopped me working.'

'You don't *have* to work now.'

'So.'
'So?'
'Just – so.'
'Just so ask a friend round. If that's the way you feel. Ask a friend round.'
'Suggestions please.'
Matt shook his watch at her.
'Lily, it's a quarter to three!'
Madam's arms were now akimbo. A bad sign.
'So whom do you suggest I ask round? I'm not allowed to invite Jenny because she puts cigarette ends down the nessy – '
'Of course you can ask Jenny round.'
'No I can't. Val's Verboten since she voted for the National Front.'
'Quite right, too. The woman's a fascist!'
'She only did it for a joke, Matt.'
'Ha, ha.'
'Marianne's banned because she doesn't say anything and Sheila's banned because she says too much. You don't like Diana because she's a redhead – '
'Red haired women make me feel – hot.'
'And as for poor Maggie. Oi vai.'
'Poor Maggie my back teeth.'
'Matt, there is nothing *wrong* in breast feeding.'
'Of course there isn't! But not in Sainsbury's!'
'I suppose it did cause a bit of a stir, didn't it?'
'Stir? I should think they're still talking about it on the butter counter. She's a big girl, Lily.'
Lily looked at him.
'So who can I have round about whom you will not go completely spare?'
'Have who you like. But can we please get some sleep?'
'How can I sleep when I have no friends?'
This last was said with the proper hint of Jokasta.
'You want your friends to come round here and sleep with us as well.'
'Oh – c'est extra indeed! My friends aren't allowed round here.'
'Of course your friends are allowed round here!'
'Such as?'
'Such as anybody you care to ask!'

Lily opened her eyes wide as saucers. Well nearly.

'Maggie?' she asked 'innocently'.

'No – not Maggie. Anybody but Mother Earth Maggie.'

'Val? Marianne? Sheila? Jenny?'

Matt gritted his teeth and then tried to speak through them.

'Anybody you like. Except Val, Marianne, Sheila, Jenny – or – '

'Mother Earth Maggie.'

'Yes.'

Lily's eyes narrowed, but she sensed there was victory lying around somewhere.

'Mmm. Limits the field a bit.'

She lay back.

'Now put out your light, and can we get some sleep?'

Lily clicked her tongue, but she put out her light. As if that was going to make any difference. Just because her light was out did not mean that she was going to give up. Oh no.

'It's all right for you – '

'*What* is all right for me now?'

'Nothing.'

Silence, and then, 'You can have round who you like.'

'I don't *have* anybody round!'

'That's because you don't like anybody.'

'Lily!'

Bull's eye. Straight slam in the middle. Total silence while she contemplated her dart in the middle of the board. It made it all worth while somehow, to score like that. She was just about to drop off to sleep, when it hit her.

'GEORGE!'

Matt, who too had been just about to drop off to sleep, now fell out of bed. He picked himself up off the floor and wearily climbed back in again, before asking the relevant question.

'George? George who?'

Not boyfriends now, surely?

'Oh nobody. Georgina Chubb. We were at secretarial school together.'

'Fascinating.'

'I'm sure Diana said she was back from Italy. And she's not on the black list.'

'Yet,' muttered Matt darkly.

'If she is back, I've a good mind to ask her round to dinner,' continued Lily smoothly, in that particular 'I haven't heard what you just said' kind of way that women can do so well.

'You will *not* ask her round for dinner! I come home to dinner. Dinner and the evening is – it's *our* time.'

'Well, you're just going to have to share it for once, Mussolini. It's all right. You'll like George. Oh I do hope she's back from Italy.'

She turned her light off – Boadicea triumphant.

Matt turned off his and then found it was now he who was lying awake staring at the ceiling, while Lily drifted off in to a peaceful slumber. Georgina Chubb indeed. Georgina Chubb. He hated her already.

A few days later, the fateful day when he knew that Lily's so-called friend was being asked to dinner, Matt contrived to linger longer than usual at the recording studio. He wasn't at his best with human beings en masse, and if anything, even worse than ever at being on his own with them – except Lily of course, but if there was one thing he could not abide at all it was Lily and a Friend. It wasn't something that he felt that his life and marriage was about. Sharing Lily with her mother was bad enough, but sharing Lily with a friend was torture. Particularly since most of her friends were such fiends. They always turned out to be the sort of girls he couldn't stand, married to the sort of men he couldn't stand and living the sort of lives that would in his opinion be intolerable to a worm.

He opened his front door with a heavy heart. He could smell the familiar scent of small, cheap, cigarettes that always filled their one and a half rooms when a 'friend' was in. Not only that but he could hear Lily giggling that particular 'all girls together' sort of giggle that she only put on when she was with one of Them. Not only that, but Lily would most probably have completely forgotten that he, Matt, needed feeding, and there would probably be one of those 'oh darling I thought you'd eaten' exchanges which would make him feel not only unwanted, but worse than unwanted – unfed.

'Hallo Matt.'

'Hallo Lily.'

He avoided looking at Her Friend.

'This is George,' said Lily crisply.

'Hallo George,' said Matt evenly, and put down his brief case.

He thought she said 'hallo' back, but since after that it was straight back to the chat, chat, giggle, giggle, she might as well not have bothered. Honestly, you wouldn't believe what women found to talk about. It wasn't until the lamb cutlets that he even managed to get a *word* in, and then it was completely edgeways.

'So there we were, walking along this amazing Via del Tritone, you really must go to Italy, Lil – '

Lily waved her fork at Matt.

'We really must go to Italy, Matt.'

'We really must *not* go to Italy, Lily.'

'It is amazing. And round the corner who should come zapping along but you'll never guess Toad and the awful Harry the Yawn. Wasn't that amazing?'

'Amazing.'

It was Matt's turn to wave his fork.

'Extraordinary.'

Lily leant forward to cut off his view.

'You do mean Teresa Toad from Totteridge with those funny ears and the hair on her back?'

'*Yes* – anyway it was *she* who told me about Helen – you remember Helen and the transvestite prince.'

Lily crossed her fingers and waved them at George.

'Which reminds me – '

George looked at her.

'You have *heard* about Helen and the transvestite prince?'

Another wave of the crossed fingers.

'I mustn't forget to tell you about Mary Talbot and her teeth.'

'You see Helen had met this amazing prince – so called – ha-ha-ha who was actually a princess – in Naples where they'd just come back from – '

Matt leant across Lily.

'I hope I'm not boring you?' he asked heavily. But it made no difference to the flow. Madam still carried on. The woman was made of granite.

'*I* was going to Naples but then they had this amazing outbreak of cholorea – '

'Cholera,' Matt corrected.

'Sssh.'

Lily frowned reprovingly.

'Sorry I spoke.'

Lily frowned again. Really Matt was quite impossible, he just couldn't keep out of things.

'But of course,' continued George, 'when I heard about it – '

'Sorry for being alive.'

Lily frowned harder at Matt. As for being sorry he was alive, well quite frankly just at the minute he wasn't the only one who was sorry he was alive.

'Well, you know what I'm like, me and my health. Well when I heard about the cholera – '

'Chol*orea*,' quoth Mr Clever-Clever.

'Will you sssshhh.'

This time Lily tried kicking him under the table.

'I just dropped everything.'

'A very dangerous thing to do in Italy.'

This was too much. Both girls turned slowly and looked at him. Really he was the end.

'Go on George,' said Lily heavily, her eyes still pinning Matt down.

'I just dropped everything,' George continued, 'and zapped up to Florence where I bought these *shoes*.'

All eyes down to the shoes.

'Oh aren't they terrific?'

'Aren't they amazing,' agreed George happily.

'Aren't they shoes?' asked Matt.

Lily's eyes once more threw a thousand poisoned arrows in Matt's direction.

'Matt,' she said slowly, 'why don't you go and make the coffee?'

But not a million poisoned arrows could make Mr Browne give up his position of attack.

'Doesn't anybody want to hear what I did this morning?' he asked innocently.

The girls' eyes left him, and re-directed themselves towards George's shoes again.

'I saw exactly the same pair in Bond Street for exactly twice the price, Lil, and they weren't even the *same*.'

'I got on the bus, paid my exact fare exactly, get off the bus at the exact stop exactly – '

'Matt – go and make some coffee.'

'And they didn't even have these little buckles,' George finished triumphantly.

'And then I got to the recording studios, hung around for three hours, got on the bus and came home again.'

Matt too finished, but not in such triumphant style.

'I should imagine,' said Lily through gritted teeth, 'they're queuing up for the film rights. Now go and make the *coffee*.'

Matt went, glaring. From behind the plastic curtain that divided Lily and George from him and the kitchen he could hear Lily asking George, 'Why are you back so soon? Jenny said you were going to stay out there for a year.'

'My *glands*, Lil.'

'Oh not your *glands* again, George?'

'I can't help my glands, Lil.'

Matt made a noise between a groan and a screech and started to clear up the kitchen, which was completely necessary if he was going to be able even to boil the kettle, let alone prepare the coffee. Honestly – women! When they weren't going on about their shoes, or their wretched glands, they were leaving things everywhere. *Look* at all this mess Lily had left – would you just look? Make-up beside the coffee pot, coffee pot beside the toast rack.

'I'm so amazingly susceptible to everything that's going round, Lil,' came from outside the plastic curtain.

Matt banged the kettle on the stove.

You bet she was. Girls like her always were susceptible to everything, and then of course they had to go round letting the whole world know, as if the whole world would even be remotely interested in the fact that she was susceptible to disease when, if he was anything to go by, the whole world would be nothing if not delighted that she caught things easily. In fact as far as he was concerned, the best thing she could do would be to catch something here and now, but pronto.

He poured the hot water on the coffee.

'Anyway. What's the flat situation like round here, Lil? I've got to find somewhere pretty soon.'

'It's un peu hairy as a matter of fact, George. But you could always kip here, until you find somewhere.'

She could always *what*? Susceptible George kipping here in their nest. He picked up Lily's lipstick from the table. Oh no, oh no, oh no, no, Mrs Browne, not if it were ever so.

'Coffee?'

Matt laid the tray gracefully down in front of the girls.

'Matt!'

'Sugar and cream, Georgina?'

'Matt, what on earth's that all up your arm?'

'Sorry?'

'Matt what on earth are those spots?'

'SPOTS!'

'And look – he's got them all over his chest as well!'

'What?'

Matt stared down at himself as if noticing for the first time.

'Oh no,' he gasped. 'It's that damned double bass player.'

'What on *earth* are they?'

Georgina started to edge towards the door.

'Fantamoritis,' whispered Matt. 'And he swore it wasn't infectious.'

'Matt – they're *huge*.'

Lily leant forward. Visions of months and months spent nursing Matt and bringing him bunches of grapes floated before her eyes. Matt backed away from her.

'No don't touch them! If you touch them they – they leave terrible scars!'

Georgina was half way out of the door by now.

'Look, look Lil – '

Matt turned to her.

'This poor double bass player had them all over his face,' he said dramatically.

'Lil,' Georgina murmured, 'I think I'd better split. What with my susceptibilities and everything – '

'It might be the best thing,' said Matt regretfully.

'I think you'd better, George,' Lily agreed 'But you must come round as soon as this clears up. This – whatever it is.'

'I'll ring you. Ciaou.'

Lily looked at the closed door.

'Oh môche. Quel domage,' she sighed.

She turned to Matt.

'Just as we were getting on so well too,' he said.

Suddenly Lily's eyes narrowed. There was something about dear hubby that she couldn't put her finger on, a certain element of the cat having swallowed the cream. Et cetera, et cetera.

'Matt?'

'Mmmm?'

'Let me see those spots.'

'No, no, no. You mustn't come near.'

But she was too quick for him and as he tried to dodge behind the sofa she caught his arm.

'Well, well, well,' she said looking down at the 'spots'. 'You caught this off your bass player, did you?'

'Yes.'

'Pretty funny bass player, Matt. And next time you see him you can give him a message from me.'

Matt's eyes widened.

'I can?'

Lily nodded.

'Tell him I don't think Blushing Peach is quite his shade.'

Basically that might have been the end of that, if Lily had not been made of sterner stuff. Another girl, faced with a nearest and dearest who would rather cover himself with pretend spots than sit through an evening shared with someone else, another girl might have given in, but not this one. Lily Pond from Streatham might not look as if she was able to stand up to Matthew Browne Esquire, but she was personally out to prove that looks were deceptive. Q.E.D. Or put that in your proverbial pipe and smoke it, M. Browne. The very next day she rang up Georgina and asked her round again. And not many days after that, George did indeed re-appear.

'So you found a flat all right?'

'Hardly a flat, Lil. More like a figment of a landlord's imagination. Hey – and guess who I saw on my flat-searching travels? Gerald the crooked dentist.'

'You didn't.'

'I did. And he sent you a big kiss.'

Lily giggled.

'Oh môche. Whatever you do don't mention Gerald in front of Matt.'

'Why? Is he funny about people you've been out with?'

'No. No, he's just funny about people I've been out with. He's funny about people I *haven't* been out with.'

Lily peered at the sauce she was concocting, and then added philosophically, 'He's just funny about people full stop.'

George leant against the kitchen curtain.

'Tell me, what songs has your Matt written? Anything I might have hummed in the bath?'

'Depends whether or not you're a fan of Cracko Dogfood, Sunshine detergent or Wibby's Wonderbras.'

'He writes jingles, does he?'

'At the moment. To pay the rent. He's working on some songs as well.'

George let the curtain drop and a few seconds later Lily heard the rumble of a boogey starting up – on Matt's piano!

'You'd better not let Matt catch you,' she said nervously.

But George just shrugged her elegant shoulders and went on boogying.

Unfortunately for Lily just at that precise moment Matt, who had hitherto been humming his way up the corridor towards his front door, quickly dropped the hum and started to hurry towards the aforesaid front door. If he was not mistaken, and he very much wished he was, if he was *not* much mistaken there was someone in *his* flat, sitting at his piano PLAYING IT! Daddy Bear flung open the front door and, without waiting to close it, he strode across the room and slammed down the lid of the piano.

'That is not a vehicle for vamping. That is a Steinway E,' he growled at George. It *would* have to be George.

'I know,' said George softly, 'it's nearly as nice as our old Bluthner as played by Scarlatti.'

'You might at least have said hallo to George, Matt.'

'Hallo George,' said Matt obediently, to Lily's astonishment.

'Hi Matt. Glad to hear you're better.'

Matt nodded down at her.

'Better?' he asked absent-mindedly.

'The spotted effect.'

'Oh yes, the spotted effect. Yes, I'm much better thanks.'

Looking down at George he suddenly realised there was more to her than he had at first realised. A lot more to her.

'You actually have a Bluthner that was actually played by Scarlatti.'

'My family does.'

Georgina nodded.

'Amazing,' said Matt.

And he sat down beside her.

'Amazing.'

There was a short pause as Lily realised that Matt had actually sat down beside George, and then she said tentatively, 'Er – George is staying for supper, Matt.'

'Your family piano was actually played by Scarlatti?' repeated Matt slowly.

'Right.'

'So er – that's all right then? If George stays for – er supper?' squeaked Lily uncertainly.

Matt turned to her impatiently.

'Lily, stop rabbiting and ask your friend George if she'd like to stay for supper.'

Lily pulled a face over his head at Georgina.

'You can read that as welcome on the Matt.'

She disappeared into the kitchen and, once behind the curtain, she found herself smiling at nothing in particular, and everything in general. It was, after all, so nice when your husband got on with one of your friends. Something she had always wanted was now happening, Matt and George, Lily's friend, were getting on like a house on fire. Three cheers for everything. She started to prepare supper in the certain knowledge that they would both be able to sit and chat to each other without any more to do.

And that's exactly what happened. They both sat and chatted to each other. They chatted through the crisps and sherry before supper, they chatted through the egg-and-bacon-flan-with-new-potatoes-and-peas. They chatted through the two half bottles of white wine she'd put away for a rainy day, they chatted and chatted as if neither of them had ever met anybody else who was interested in music ever before.

'No, it wasn't!'

'Yes, it was! And it was his first big concert, remember?'

'Yes, you're right! Of course it was.'

'And Bernstein was the conductor.'

Lily held up a small hand.

'Anyone for pudding?'

'Sssh. I'm telling a story.'

Matt shook his head reprovingly at Lily.

'It's gooseberry fool.'

'Lily. Please. Where was I?'

'Zoltowski was the conductor,' said George sympathetically.

'Right. So they finish the piano concerto and off they both go to the wings.'

Lily put up her hand again.

'It's homemade.'

'Whereupon Zoltowski pushes the young pianist back towards the stage and urges him to go out and take a solo bow. Of course the audience goes mad.'

Up went Lily's hand again.

'The gooseberries are fresh.'

'And back he goes again to the wings. And Zoltowski pushes him back out by himself again. In fact he pushes him out for four solo bows, and, of course, our young virtuoso can't believe it. This great conductor being so unselfish. So there he finally stands, back in the wings with the audience roaring for more, when he feels Zoltowski tap him on the shoulder. "Right," says Zoltowski in his ear, "now drag me on." '

Georgina clapped her hands in approval.

'Amazing!'

Matt laughed.

'Isn't it amazing?'

'Amazing,' said Lily dourly. 'I don't understand it.'

Matt turned to her.

'I thought you were meant to be getting the gooseberry fool!'

'I,' said Lily flinging down her napkin, 'think I *am* the gooseberry fool.'

'So,' said George ignoring Lily and covering Matt's hand lightly with her own. 'So you were going to be a concert pianist, were you?'

'I was. Until I found I couldn't face the music.'

George looked tenderly puzzled.

'I'm not with you.'

'No,' growled Lily, 'I'm with him.'

'Sssh,' said Matt.

'Face the music?'

'People. Whenever I had to appear in front of large audiences – I couldn't. Talk about having to be dragged on.'

By this time Lily was in the kitchen banging everything she could see. Sacre nom d'un pipe, this was too much. She seized the gooseberry fool. She'd like to throw it all over both of them. Music buffs, honestly – they were enough to make you uncle dick.

'Talking about not appearing – you must have heard about the Silver Lining's concert in Rome, didn't you? You must have.'

'No? Oh, but remind me to tell you about the time Maria Fantini inhaled her tenor's moustache.'

Lily banged the fool down between them and 'smiled'. 'Pudding?'

George waved it aside.

'I couldn't, Lil. I've laughed too much.'

'Neither could I, Lily, I'm full.'

Lily's lip wobbled slightly.

'I made it specially.'

Matt leant across to George.

'Sorry George, what were you saying?'

'It's your favourite, Matt.'

'Sssh, Lily.'

'And I put hundreds and thousands all over it.'

Matt looked up at her briefly.

'Lily, perhaps your friend would like some coffee?'

Lily nodded slowly.

'Perhaps my friend would like some coffee,' she agreed carefully.

'Some coffee would be great.'

'Then I will go and make some coffee for my friend. And some for George as well,' she added quietly.

'Anyway – this concert in Rome.'

'BLACK OR WHITE COFFEE?' yelled Lily.

Matt and George jumped out of their seats and looked up at Sergeant Major Pond.

'What's the matter? What are you shouting for, Lily?'

'For what am I shouting? Because I wasn't sure you'd hear. Black or white coffee?'

'Black please, Lily.'

'Black would be amazing,' agreed George.

And that wasn't the only thing that would be black if she had much more of George's hand-covering techniques. Lily charged back into the kitchen.

'Oh – marbles!'

A minute later she went back into the sitting room again, only to find them both at the piano, with Matt singing to

HER. And not just singing any old song to HER but singing her's, Lily's, song to HER.

'That is – lovely,' said George soulfully as Matt finished.

'That is – my song,' said Lily quietly.

Matt nodded.

'It's a song I wrote for Lily.'

'You've never played that to anybody else,' said Lily even more quietly.

'I wrote it for Lily,' said Matt again.

'That's *my* song.'

Lily banged the coffee tray down on the piano.

'Not on the piano, Lily.'

What on earth had got into her?

'Oh,' said Lily molto forte, 'I thought you'd stopped being so fussy about what you allowed on your piano.'

Matt led George over to the sofa, leaving Lily to follow.

'Let's have it over here. And you were going to tell me all about the time you met Stephen Stills.'

'Funny you should mention the time – '

Lily banged down the tray for a second time.

Matt glanced up at her.

'Lily – you've forgotten the sugar.'

Exit Lily in search of sugar. Sugar, sugar, sugar, she'd soon sugar them. The pigs. The musical snobs. The cosy self-satisfied beasts. Them and their musical stories, honestly, she'd rarely had a worse evening. And just look at herself. She was all manky, and haggard, if not haggard and manky. Mascara smudged, lipstick worn away, nose as shiny as a beacon. She looked like the 'dry ends lank hair?' advertisement.

'Will you just look at me?' she asked herself out aloud. 'I look like the wreck of the *Hesperus*. DO you know something, Lily? You look – '

She stopped muttering suddenly and smiled at herself.

'You don't look at all well. In fact I'm rather worried about you altogether.'

Her smile grew wider and she picked up her 'Blushing Pink' lipstick.

When she re-emerged from the kitchen Matt and George were still cosily chatting on the sofa. George was in full flight.

'It was quite amazing. I was the first person in Addlestone to get Asian Flu. Out of all those people it had to be me.

I honestly thought I was *dying*. I had a temperature of a hundred and one for a *week*. And all my toes went numb.'

'Amazing.'

'Not only that, Matt,' again George's hand came down and covered Matt's – 'not only that but do you know that I'm one of the few people to have had chicken pox three times?'

'But I've had it three times too! Isn't that amazing?'

'It certainly is,' agreed Lily softly. 'Sugar?'

'Lily!'

Matt sprang to his feet and stared at his wife aghast.

'Lily – what on earth is the matter with you?'

'Well,' said Lily carefully, 'you know that infection you had? I seem to have caught it too.'

Two pairs of eyes travelled over Lily's face, and down her shoulders and arms. She was covered in large red spots just the same as Matt had had, only if anything hers were slightly larger. Lily looked from George to Matt and back again. Fantomoritis anyone?

CHAPTER NINE

'Make Them Listen – Croon Anywhere'

It was a boiling hot day. Not at all the sort of weather to be sitting in the outer office of a musical agent's apartment seeking an interview. Matt stopped trying to transform the stain on the carpet in front of him into the face of Holmes, the bully at his prep school, and turned his attention to the hideous wallpaper, most of which, thank heavens, was masked by equally hideous posters advertising hideously untalented people who had quite obviously – judging from the opulence of the surroundings – made 'HARRY BURTON MUSICAL AGENT INC.' hideously rich. Such was the way of the world. Still, at least Harry Burton had a stain on his carpet. That was the good thing. Not even being as rich as H. Burton Esq. could stop stains arriving on your carpet.

The secretary nodded at Matt.

'Okay!'

'Okay?'

She jerked her head towards the great man's door.

'You can go in,' she said, and stuck her chewing gum in the ashtray as Matt walked past.

Slut, thought Matt loudly, as he prepared to enter the portals of the great man.

'Six minutes.'

Harry Burton did not look up at Matt as he came in but continued to pursue the occupation that had obviously had him enthralled for some time, namely playing with his 'executive toy', a nasty object made up of steel balls.

'I'm sorry?'

Harry Burton tapped a timer on his desk with one hand.

'I can give six minutes.'

'Six minutes? Perhaps I should come back another day when you're not so busy.'

'Today I am less busy. Otherwise would you be here? Speak.'

'Speak?'

'Who are you?'

'Oh. Who am I. I'm – my name is Matthew Browne, I'm a composer and I'm looking for somebody to represent my interests.'

'And what makes you interesting?'

'My music. Didn't you get my tape?'

'You sent me a tape?'

'Yes, look – here it is.'

Matt picked it up off the desk.

'Haven't you listened to it?'

'Refresh my tired memory. Tingle my jaded palate.'

Matt put the tape on the cassette player. Harry Burton listened to it for a few seconds and then nodded wisely, ' "Red Sails in the Sunset",' he pronounced.

' "Red Sails in the Sunset"?'

'La, lala-la la – "Red Sails in the Sunset". It's been done, son.'

'These are all originals, I assure you.'

'The last original song I heard I've forgotten.'

Matt shook his head and turned the tape over.

'This is my latest. It's called "November Sky".'

Again Harry Burton listened to it for a few bars, and again he pronounced.

' "Slow Boat to China",' he said firmly.

'It is nothing like "Slow Boat to China".'

'To me it is *exactly* like "Slow Boat to China", and that's what I'm paid for – my *ear*.'

'Your ear my foot!'

Just as Matt had pronounced, a bell went off on Harry Burton's desk.

'And what's *that*.'

Harry held out a free hand and without looking up from his executive toy said, 'Been nice talking to you. Have a good day.'

'Have a good day? I've only just arrived,' Matt protested.

'Six minutes. Your allotted span.'

'It's not much of a span is it? Six minutes? I hardly consider that a fair crack of the whip.'

For the first time during the interview Harry Burton looked at Matt.

'Son,' he said, 'it's always the girl who can't dance who says the band can't play. Come back when I need you.'

Matt retraced his steps down the brown linoleum stairs out to the street, where Lily was going to meet him. That had been practically an all time record – six minutes. Lily would hardly be at their meeting place, having expected him to be at least half an hour with the wretched H. Burton, Esquire. Matt paced up and down. 'Red Sails in the Sunset' indeed! When Lily eventually arrived he said ' "Red Sails in the Sunset" indeed!' So she knew at once where she was.

'Don't tell me. Not another come-back-when-you're-famous routine?'

'He hadn't even listened to my tape, Lily. I don't know why I bother.'

'You bother because we have to get you marketed, that's why you bother. You don't promote yourself properly, that's your trouble, Buster. What you need is a bit of bizz-azz.'

'I don't know what you're rabbiting about. Bizz-azz! They wouldn't notice it if it hit them between the eyes,' Matt grumbled.

'Look – bizz-azz.'

Lily unzipped her little cotton anorak. Across her delicious frontispiece was emblazoned the words 'MAKE IT A MATTHEW BROWNE WORLD'.

'Lily!'

She turned round for him to admire the back of her tee shirt upon which was written large and red 'MAKE LOVE TO MATTHEW BROWNE'.

'Lily! Will you put your jacket back on at *once*!'

Of course she didn't. To put her jacket back on would have been as impossible for Lily as to give up this frantic idea that if no one else would promote Matt, then she would.

The next hour in his life was not one which Matt found easy to recall without his toes curling up extremely tight. Lily, convinced that she was on just the right tack to promote her husband's career, walked up and down pointing to her tee shirt every time some poor innocent passed her by, and then not content with displaying herself like a bill board, turned to community singing. She sang on the way to catch their bus, she sang at the bus stop, she sang on the bus, and when they got off again, and after every rendering of every one of his numbers, she told anyone and everyone that that was a MATTHEW BROWNE number she had just been singing, with the inevitable result that most of the bus passengers decided to walk the rest of the way home, and even the conductor spent the whole journey on the top deck.

Matt carefully shut the flat door before giving vent to his feelings.

'I have never been so embarrassed in all my life!'

'Why? I don't know why. They've all gone their separate ways as happy as sand boys doing *what*? Singing one of *your songs*.'

'I haven't actually sold any of my songs for them to buy, Lily.'

Matt flung his brief case on to the sofa.

'Of course you haven't but this is how you will! You see, if we can get people humming your tunes, singing them on buses, et cetera, et cetera, what's the next thing they'll do? I'll tell you.'

'I thought you would,' said Matt gloomily.

'They'll be queueing up at their record shops and writing into their favourite radio programme and asking for a MATTHEW BROWNE number, because of this overwhelming popular demand we'll have created.'

'Lily, Lily, will you just stop it. Just stop it and leave my career to me will you?'

'Why? I'm your partner remember? I want to help you.'

'How can *you* help me?'

'Because I believe in you – that's how I can help you.'

Matt sighed.

'You don't know anything about the music business, or about pop or about anything,' he said gently.

'Yes I do.'

Lily stuck out her chin determinedly.

'No you don't. Until I told you, you thought that the Rolling Stones was a place of interest in the Cotswolds and that Englebert Humperdink was a type of Swiss cheese. You wouldn't know a pop star if one fell on you.'

Lily looked at him. She wasn't going to go on and let him turn her promotion efforts into a subject for what was always known at Streatham as a 'Family Discussion'. The last thing a man who was out of work and disillusioned would want was a Family Discussion, but even so she was determined to help Matt in whatever way she could. She hadn't read her show biz biographies for nothing. It was well known that behind every great career there was a Good Woman and as far as she was concerned she was Matt's and, even if he didn't feel in need of her, she was in need of him.

This was the subject of their conversation the next day at breakfast.

'I still think I could be allowed to do *something*.'

'Do something about what?'

Matt looked up briefly from the Spot the Ball competition on the back of the cereal packet.

'About managing your career. Honestly I didn't get married to sit around all day with a duster on my head getting a large British Botty. You might at least let me do *something*. Mightn't he?' she asked Jacky who was busy spitting pips at Matt from his cage.

Matt picked up one of Jacky's pips and threw it back at him.

'You can do something,' he said, 'you can take this cassette of my songs to Tape Transcriptions in Richmond and order six more copies.'

'Okay, but it'll have to be after I've delivered these lovebirds for Mr Martin.'

Mr Martin was Lily's old boss from the pet shop and he'd been suffering terribly from his feet in the hot weather, so she had promised to help him out with deliveries.

'Good, well if you can do that without undue incident, who knows I might even let you run my bath tonight.'

'Oink, oink.'

Lily snorted and Matt blew her a kiss.

'Do you know something, Jacky boy?' Lily asked after he had gone. 'I think he's feeling better already.'

Mr Martin's delivery had to be delivered to a Mr Powell in Putney. It was a large posh flat on the second floor, and Lily was quite happy to find herself outside Mr Powell's door because lovebirds might be a romantic gift, but delivering them was somewhat less so. She rang the bell. From inside she could hear the strains of some dreadful Country and Western song.

The door opened and a sleepy looking face looked out at her.

'Oh hello,' said Lily brightly, 'two lovebirds for a Mr Clive Powell.'

'Speaking,' said Mr Sleepy Face.

'Eh voilà. Mr Martin says sorry they weren't ready for you yesterday, and he hopes they're in time for your wife's birthday. Okay?'

'They're in plenty of time. Won't you come in?'

'What? Oh no thanks all the same.'

'Thank *you.*'

Lily was just about to turn on her heel, when she remembered the contents of her carrier.

'Except I'd better, come in that is. I've got to give you all their stuff. You know – toothbrushes, slippers, sandsheets, that sort of thing.'

She entered the large living room which was filled by a grand piano, leather sofas, and a shifty looking man by the tape recorder. As she unpacked the stuff for the lovebirds, the shifty-looking man said, 'Pity you're not with it son, because believe you me, this is where it's *at.*'

Mr Powell didn't appear to hear what he said, because he just went on smiling at Lily and didn't answer.

'That's it I think.'

Lily started to re-pack her carrier, with all its usual paraphernalia – a thing for picking stones out of horses' hooves, a pound of ripe plums, face cream, suntan oil, three library books, Matt's tapes, in it all went again.

'Oh – one more thing, Mr Martin says best to cover them at night – because old Charlie boy here is a bit of an Errol Flynn. Know what I mean?'

'Thank you very much.'

Lily smiled.

'All part of the service. T.T.F.N.'

Exit Lily, to Mr Powell's great regret. He turned round to look at Harry Burton who had been boring him stiff for the past half hour.

'So,' said Harry brightly.

'So,' said Powell.

'This is where it's at, Georgie, or do you prefer Clive?'

Georgie Fame stroke Clive Powell shrugged his shoulders.

'Please yourself. My friends call me Clive – the public call me Georgie.'

'Well – Clive/Georgie this is where it's really at. You should hear this just *one* more time.'

Harry picked up another of the tapes from the piano and stuck it on the cassette player. If only he could get this fellow Georgie Fame to buy one of his clients' songs, it would be just terrific. T for terrific, M for money. The music flooded the room. Harry waved his foot out of time to it.

'Wait a minute.'

Georgie Fame held up a surprised hand.

Pop stars get played things at them all the time, but this had something.

'This isn't what you played before.'

'Of course it isn't what I played before, this is – I don't know what this is.'

'It's good, very good.'

'But it's good, very good,' agreed Harry hastily.

'Who's it by?'

'Who's it by? Who's it by? He doesn't know who it's by. It's by Matthew Browne, that's who it's by. Matthew Browne.'

'He's one of your clients?' asked Georgie.

'Of course he's one of my clients,' agreed Harry bravely.

And if he wasn't now, he soon would be.

The stain on Harry Burton's carpet still looked exactly like that bully Holmes. Matt stared down at it. He had no idea why this dreadful man should suddenly want to see him again so soon after he had so spectacularly failed to interest him two days ago, but when you're out of work there's very little time for speculation. You get a phone call, you go. In fact that was one of the worst features of being out of work, the startling contrast between your own eagerness and everyone else's boredom.

The secretary – former slut of two days ago – attempted to dazzle Matt with her smile.

'Mr Burton's *so* sorry for keeping you waiting, and he can see you now.'

Matt nodded, and walked past her. He wasn't sure which was worse – her being nice or her being rude.

Harry Burton held out an eager hand.

'Mr Browne. My dear Mr Browne. Come in. Come in. Have a drink. Whisky?'

'Thank you.'

'So nice to see you again. So nice to see you again. May I call you Mutt?'

'Matt would be preferable.'

'Matt – of course.'

He handed Matt a large Scotch. Matt looked at him.

'It's got a lot warmer since we last met wouldn't you say?'

Harry's hands spread out before him in a remarkable gesture of conciliation, forgiveness and understanding.

'I am so sorry about our previous confabulation. But problems. Problems. An agent's life – alas – is not an easy one.'

'But the money helps.'

'The money helps. The money helps. I like it. I like it. Which reminds me. This *great* music of yours.'

'Ah, you've listened to my tape then, have you?'

'Why not? Why not? If we don't listen we don't buy.'

Matt took out one of the tapes Lily had had transcribed for him, and pressed it on to the cassette. The room became flooded with dreadful Country and Western music. Harry nodded happily and his foot swung up and down out of time.

'This isn't my tape.'

Matt stopped the music.

'I must have picked up the wrong tape.'

'Of course it isn't. This isn't your tape.'

'I don't write Country and Western.'

'Of course you don't. Who does?'

'I must have picked up the wrong tape.'

'You see Country and Western's finished. It's all washed up. It's contemporary and contemporary's old-fashioned. We've got to get into the modern sound, so I've drawn up a contract for you, here it is, and you sign up with me and we will make music.'

He stuck a pen in Matt's hand, and indicated where to sign on the contract that had suddenly appeared from nowhere.

'A contract? Well now, I'll have to consider this, Mr Burton.'

'Mutt, consideration is the father of deprivation. Harry Burton knows a modern talent when it walks into his office.'

'All the same I'd like to take it home and read it.'

'Read it? If you're short of something to read, I can lend you a book.'

'I'd just like to read it through. I mean twenty-five per cent to me and seventy-five per cent to you?'

'That is the standard arrangement, Mutt. Would it help if I tell you *Georgie Fame* is interested in your music?'

'Georgie Fame?'

'And not only interested Mutt – *very* interested.'

Matt stared at him.

'It might help,' he said slowly, 'it might help considerably.'

Lily hummed happily round the flat. Bustling about setting out nuts, and crisps, and even placing a festive bunch of roses in the middle of the coffee table. Just wait till Matt got home! What a story she had to tell him! Mind you she nearly didn't have a story to tell him. It could have been dreadful, the whole business. Imagine getting Mr Powell's tapes muddled up with Matt's? Supposing he had been someone dreadful who had just thrown them away or something? Matt would never have forgiven her. But not only had he *not* been someone dreadful, Mr Powell had turned out to be someone incredibly important in the music world who had acquired an incredibly deep fascination in Matt's music – on account of her having left the tapes on his piano – and now here he was coming round this evening with a view to discussing *buying* one of Matt's songs. Talk about zipperty do-dah, zipperty-day.

'Oh Matt! Matt have I got some news for you.'

'And have I got some news for you.'

Matt thrust another bunch of roses at her. Lily looked from him to the roses and back again.

'You haven't crashed my bike again have you?'

'Lily, those come with love and no guilt.'

'Matt – they're beautiful. Are you sure you haven't crashed my bike again?'

'Lily I have bought you a present.'

'Why did you buy me a present?'

'Because somebody is interested in my *music*.'

'How did you know?'

'Because Harry Burton told me.'

'What did he tell you?'

'Wait till you hear, wait till you hear who's interested. Only *Georgie Fame.*'

'Who's Georgie Fame?'

'Who's – Lily I told you you knew nothing about this business. He's one of the top singers in the whole country.'

'Is he?'

'Apparently Harry Burton played him my tape and he went over the moon. Not only that but he's coming round this evening to talk to me about an *exclusive contract.*'

'He is?'

'Any minute now. So you organise the drinks while I have a quick Bob Squash.'

Exit into the bathroom to leave Lily panicking. Poor Mr Powell who was also due to be coming round would have to be metaphorically kissed good-bye. Matt popped his head back round the bathroom door.

'Lily, I'm sorry – I never asked you your news! You said you had some good news as well.'

'I did?' Lily squeaked. 'Well my news is – I haven't got any news. You know what they say – no news is good news.'

She smiled brightly at Matt. Matt shook his head.

'Who's Georgie Fame indeed – '

He went back to having his 'Bob Squash'.

As it turned out he might as well not have bothered because two and half hours later – still no sign of the famous singer.

'Perhaps he got lost?'

'If he hasn't he certainly can now,' said Matt bitterly, 'it's half past *nine.*'

'That's show business I suppose. All hot air and no balloons.'

'I should have known old Harry Burton was just mouth and trousers.'

Silence as they went back to contemplating the bitterness of life.

'There's always Mr Powell,' said Lily suddenly.

'Who on earth is Mr Powell?'

'Yes, well,' said Lily hesitatingly, 'he's the bit of news I didn't give you. You see to cut a long story short he heard your tape and he's very interested in your music, and he's in the music business as well. Or so he says. And well.'

'Well?'

'He *was* going to come round this evening, but a bit of Fame called Georgie stopped him. Mind you I could always give him a ring, and see if he's still free?'

'Of course you could!'

Matt beamed.

Having refilled the nut and crisp dishes they prepared to receive a guest for the second time that evening.

'I think it's best if you leave all the talking to me, Lily. Right?'

'Why? At least I know who he is, Matt.'

The bell rang.

'That'll be him. You just leave it all to me Cleopatra.'

Matt opened the door.

'Good heavens,' Lily heard him say. 'You're a bit late aren't you?'

'I got here as quickly as I could,' came the reply.

'Quarter past *ten*?'

Lily joined Matt at the door. There was poor Mr Powell standing there being attacked by Matt.

'*Matt!*'

Leave everything to him indeed.

'Hello. Sorry about the mix-up.'

'That's perfectly all right,' said Mr Powell affably.

'What mix-up?'

'Nothing.'

Lily gave Matt her darkest frown.

'We were expecting you a little sooner.'

'Matt – he's already said he got here as quickly as he could.'

'So.'

'So.'

'What would you like to drink – '

'Clive – '

'Georgie – '

Lily found herself frowning even harder at Matt. Honestly he couldn't even get the poor man's name right.

'Georgie?'

'Lily,' said Matt patiently, 'this is Georgie Fame.'

'Matt, this is Clive Powell.'

She turned to Mr Powell.

'Right?'

'Right. Georgie Fame's my stage name.'

'You were saying?'

Lily stamped her foot at Matt.

'Oh that is really la coming from you! You who is meant to know everything about the musical world.'

'So what are you rabbiting on about now?'

'Well you didn't know Georgie Fame's real name was Clive Powell did you?'

'No. No, I didn't,' Matt was forced to admit.

Lily started to laugh.

'No, no – well neither did I.'

CHAPTER TEN

Keeping Your Composer

The moment when a girl finds out that she is going to have a baby is, or has been, immortalised in her own imagination for years before. The moment when Lily discovered was immortalised in her memory, because far from being able to rush home from the doctor's and tell Matt, she could only walk home and tell her mother. The reason being that Matt was somewhat pregnant himself. Well, not exactly pregnant as such, but in full flight of trying to compose his first song for Georgie Fame and all in all, in Lily's opinion, it was not the time to raise his blood pressure even more by *her* news.

'I take it Matt does *want* a baby?' asked Mrs Pond.

'Of course he wants a baby. We've been talking about it and thinking about it for ages. But right now he's up to his eyelashes writing this song.'

'So what gives a song the ante-position over my first grandchild?'

'Your first grandchild's future.'

'Nothing of note has ever been said in a song.'

'No – but plenty's been sung.'

'WILL YOU PLEASE KEEP YOUR VOICES DOWN?' Matt yelled through the closed kitchen door.

Mrs Pond looked at her only daughter.

'He's been like this ever since he got the commission. And he hasn't written one note.'

Enter Matt looking miserable.

'I feel sick,' he announced dramatically from the door.

'He's like this every morning,' said Lily.

'*He's* like this every morning,' muttered Mrs Pond.

'Where are the aspirin?'

'In the bathroom. But you shouldn't take aspirin if you've got a dodgy tum.'

'I am not taking them for my stomach, Lily. I am taking them for my back.'

He put his hand in the small of his back and went out again groaning.

'I would say you were not the only one who is polliniferous.'

Matt put his head round the door again.

'Don't bother about any lunch, Lily. Unless you're going out.'

'Why? Is there anything you particularly fancy?'

'No – yes. It's ridiculous but I have this craving for some pineapple and raspberry jam.'

Mrs Pond waved a finger at Lily.

'And you think I'm joking?'

Once more Tom was called in for a diagnosis of his brother-in-law's condition and once more Tom remained baffled by his symptoms.

'Off your normal diet, absurd craving, back ache, morning sickness. If I didn't know you better, Matt, I'd say you were pregnant.'

'What are you talking about?'

Matt leapt up from the bed.

'I am simply in the middle of a creative spasm.'

'Ah well. I cer-can't prescribe for ther-that, I'm afraid.'

'Of course you can't. And why not? Because I am stuck, stuck, stuck. And why am I stuck? Because I don't know what to write about!'

Tom looked at Lily.

'I have to ger-go and finish my rounds. Rather you than me, Sis!'

'Hear, hear,' said Lily morosely. 'I'm beginning to get an idea of how Mrs Beethoven felt.'

She shut the front door and turned to Matt who was still moodily pacing.

'Now then.'

'What's all this "now then"?'

'Just – nothing. Just – "now then". Now then I was going to organise you, that's all.'

'I do not need organising, Lily. I just need to get *on*!'

'And *now* where are you going?'

'To get your pineapple and raspberry jam.'

'I do not want pineapple and raspberry jam – I just want an idea!'

'Oh – well I'd better get on with the housework.'

'Housework!'

'Yes, remember, mop, mop, mop, Hoover, Hoover?'

'Lily, I am meant to be working.'

'Where are you going?'

'I am going out for a walk, because like Winnie the Pooh – I have lots of things to clear from my *head*.'

Lily watched him fetch his jacket and go. She felt quite miserable to see Matt so miserable. Oh dear. And what's more it appeared she was just about to be Uncle Dick.

Matt walked. And the more he walked the more he realised that half his trouble was that he hadn't done enough walking before, because possibly had he done so, he would have realised that walking was just the way to release all those pent-up feelings that hithertofore had not had expression. So, it was not surprising therefore that, after so much walking, a little something of a tune started to develop in his head. The only trouble was that although the little something was developing in his head, there was nowhere to write it down, except his shirt cuff. Oblivious to any other need except the immediate one, Matt started to write his song down – on his shirt cuff.

Naturally Lily knew nothing of this. As she swept and Hoovered and wiped and polished, she just hoped that Matt would come home with all those things that he had wanted cleared from his head – cleared. And of course in a nice ordinary way she was very glad that she happened to have decided to cook him something for his supper that was one of his 'favourites'. That is the sort of thing that can re-assure a girl who is being Uncle Dick rather more often than she cares to admit.

'Lily.'

'Matt.'

She stopped in the middle of her scrub, scrub, wash, wash, and looked up at him anxiously. Had the thousands of things that he'd had to clear from his head gone?

'I was beginning to worry about you.'

Matt smiled happily.

'Dear Lily, our worries will soon be at an end. Is the water hot?'

'Should be.'

'Good. Because I want a bath.'

Lily smiled.

'Anything you want washed? What about this shirt?'

Matt had already disappeared to flood the small bathroom with steam.

'What?' he called.

'Nothing. Water hot?'

'Boiling,' called Matt.

'You sound in great form,' said Lily.

'I certainly am, I certainly am. I think I may have got the tune for the song. Now. What did I do with my shirt?'

This last went unheard by Lily who in the middle of doing her scrub, scrub, wash, wash, had discovered that Matt had simply covered his good new shirt with Biro marks.

'Matt, Matt, how on earth did you get this Biro all over your shirt? I'll never get it off.'

Matt hummed above the sound of the bath water.

'It came to me down by the river. No – that's not quite it. But it doesn't matter, because I wrote it down on my shirt cuff.'

'Sorry?'

'I said it doesn't matter if I can't remember the tune exactly – if at all – because I wrote it down on my shirt cuff.'

These last sentences were delivered after he'd turned the taps off in the bathroom, with a consequence that they came through to Lily just as she had finished washing out his shirt, and letting out the soapy water.

'Oh no!' she whispered to herself, and then called out uncertainly to Matt, 'You wrote it down on what?'

'It's all right I wrote it down on the shirt I was wearing. Thank Heavens, I'd never remember it otherwise.'

Lily watched the last of the soapy water disappearing down the plug hole. Talk about letting the baby out with the bath water. Oh Matt. Oh Matt. What had she done?

Matt dipped one finger in the bath water. Perfect. Everything was perfect. He had the tune. Lily was cooking his favourite calves' liver with lemon and – he had the tune.

'Soap. Lily. We need some Joe Dope.'

He wandered through to the kitchen. No Lily.

'Lily? Lily?'

He found himself looking up at her 'Memory Board'. On it she had written – 'OH – MATT!' He looked down at the sink where only a minute ago she had been standing. His shirt, his good shirt, all cleanly washed out, and his song with it.

'Oh Lily. Lily?'

In most circumstances a hardworking widowed mother likes to welcome her daughter home. Mrs Pond was no exception she would quite freely admit to any of her neighbours. It was just that welcoming Lily back to Streatham in a pregnant state, and in the knowledge that Lily had in some way offended her husband, wasn't the most auspicious of home-comings. It wasn't the kind that a mother fondly imagines when she is sewing the last stitch in her daughter's wedding dress.

'You haven't touched your breakfast.'

Lily looked up at her mother and tried to smile.

'I'm not really hungry, Ma.'

'For one week you eat nothing.'

'I'm really not hungry.'

'Dogs and children never starve themselves, but sweet-hearts do.'

Lily nodded without having heard.

'I think I will ring him, Ma.'

'No you will not go and ring him. If he wanted you to ring him he'd have rung by now. I am not having any daughter of mine not answered back on the telephone.'

'He wouldn't ring me, Ma. Not after what I did to his musical shirt.'

Mrs Pond smiled.

'You make a joke. Now things will soon get better.'

'I make a joke, because if I didn't – oh why doesn't he ring?'

'He will. He'll soon ring,' said Mrs Pond determinedly, 'I've sent your brother round.'

A mother's confidence is unshakeable. Mrs Pond's confidence in her son Tom's ability to talk her son-in-law Matt into ringing her daughter Lily, was unshakeable. Along with most mothers, Mrs Pond believed that her daughter's virtue and beauty were as undeniable as her son Tom's ability to move mountains. The only flaw in this particular creed however was, as it so often is, that dreaded confuser – alcohol.

'No – no – under no circumstazzes will I call her, Tom. Under no circumstazzes. She prollaly never wanze to hear my voice again.'

'Nozzenze. She is prollally dyin for you to rin her.'

Matt considered this for a moment, and then swept the board with his reply.

'*If* she wanned me to ring *her* – she would have run *me* by now. She dozen wan me to ring, Tod.'

'Tom.'

'And can you *blame* her? If she relly thins I am the sord of persong who would, jusss because she did whad she did – Tod – '

'Tom.'

'*If* and I say if she really thins I'm thad sort of persong – '

'Which you are – '

'Thad has nothin to do with id. And if she thins thad I am thad sord of persong, then all I can say is id's liddle wonner she had left me, Tom.'

'Tod. She hazzn, she hazzn left you Madd.'

'She has lefd me, Tom. Whad am I goin to do?'

'Goan see her.'

'Whad's happened to your stammer?'

'Never mind about my stammer. Rin her up.'

'Suppose she doesn't anzer the phone because she izzn there?'

'I know wride her a ledder. Wride her a ledder.'

'A ledder? I carn wride ledders. My ledders all turn out like thinly disguised threats. I carn wride ledders. I've never bin ale to ride a ledder. One of the larse ledders I ever rode was to my mother – and she rode back to tell me our cad had died and my father had lefd home. In that order. To this day I have never been altogether sure thad my ledder and his depardure weren't inner-connected. The ledder killeth! But the spirit giveth life. What am I goan to do?'

'You're goin to ride her a ledder,' repeated Tom stubbornly.

'No I'm nod. I am nod going to ride her a letter. But you

know something, Tom. I am goin to *ride* to her. I am goin to ride somethin to Liddy.'

'Lily! Lily! A letter for you!'

Mrs Pond flew into Lily's bedroom.

'What?'

'Lily – a letter.'

'Who from? From whom? A letter? Who's it from? I mean whom's it from?'

'Isn't that Matt's writing?'

'Matt's writing? It isn't. It is. It's from Matt.'

'It's from Matt,' Mrs Pond tried to stop her voice from trembling. 'Now perhaps you'll eat.'

Two weeks, two whole weeks without a morsel taken. She had even taken to slipping Complan into her hot milk, just so she had *something* in her tummy.

Lily opened the envelope.

'It's a ticket.'

'To where?'

'To where for a show.'

'And?'

'There's no and. There's nothing with it. Just a ticket.'

This time it was Lily who was trying to stop her voice from trembling.

'And?'

'There's no and. Just a ticket.'

'And what's this ticket for?'

She peered at the card.

'Georgie Fame in concrete?'

Lily snatched it back.

'Georgie Fame in Concert, Ma.'

'So who is this famous Georgie Famous?'

'Only this famous singer who's going to do Matt's song. He must have finished it then,' she added reminiscently.

'So this is wonderful. You will be going then?'

Two weeks. Two whole weeks, and then this? She looked at her mother, furious.

'Going? Me going? I haven't heard sight nor sound of him for two whole weeks, and you ask me if I'll be going? He can't even write a letter let alone a note, let alone a line to actually ask me if I'll be going, and you ask me if I'll be going? Of course I'll be going!'

Matt didn't think anyone could feel quite as alone as he felt at that moment. Convinced that Lily wouldn't turn up, now his convictions were being substantiated. The floor manager turned to him.

'Still no sign of her I'm afraid, Matt.'

Matt nodded morosely. What a stupid plan, what an inane idea, to expect the poor girl to turn up here at the television studio to hear this wretched song sung by Georgie Fame. Why should she bother? Why should she be even remotely interested after the way he had treated her?

'Ten, nine, eight, seven – '

The countdown till when they were on the air had started.

The voice came over the studio.

'Ladies and Gentlemen – Mr Georgie Fame!'

Out comes Georgie Fame stroke Clive Powell, but not a trace of Lily Browne *née* Pond.

'Hi. It's not every day you discover a brand new song writer but can I tell you something ladies and gentlemen – today's the day. So I'm going to start the show by playing you this brand new song by this brand new song writer, and if this is anything to go by, there's a lot more where this came from. So here it is – it's called "Lily" and it's by Matthew Browne.'

'Lily! We're silly to quarrel!
Lily! It's sad we're apart!
Lily! We're acting like Laurel
And Hardy – it's breaking my heart!'

The opening bars of the song and still no Lily. Matt put his head in his hands, and there it stayed until suddenly he realised that instead of two hands holding his same head there were three. She had arrived. Lily was here.

'I couldn't have done it without you,' said Matt with uncustomary humility.

It was hours later, and they were standing alone on the set of where The Georgie Fame Hour had just been recorded.

'You did it without me, buster.'

'That's the whole point, Cleopatra.'

'So now I have to leave you every time you're composing?'

'You can leave me every time I *lose* my composure.'

'Anyway. It's not going to be quite as easy in the future. Leaving you.'

'I hope it isn't.'

'You see – because – you see – I have something to tell you.'

'Yes?'

'Well. It's not going to be so easy dans le future – '

'Yes?'

'You're so impatient. Because well. To put it another way.'

'Yes. What?'

'Just listen! Look. You and I. Toi et moi. I mean it isn't as if we haven't talked about having – and since you were and I was – and then you see I left you because I couldn't exactly tell you then – could I, because it wouldn't have been fair – not with you working so hard and anyway I wasn't there to tell you, was I? So how could I tell you? The whole point is that now – in our lives – you see, it's not just going to be you and me and – môche I had this all so well *rehearsed*.'

Matt's jaw dropped.

'You're pregnant.'

'Why don't you ever listen? What was I going to say?'

'You're going to have a *baby*?'

'Yes, that's right, but what with one thing and another, things never quite turn out as you plan them, and you don't know what's the best time to tell someone, or how to tell them, or how people are going to react and it isn't a bit like the movies – what did you say?'

'You're-going-to-have-a-baby.'

Lily stood back from him and put her hands on her hips.

'Well. Isn't that typical? You might at least have let *me* tell you!'

THE END